CW01080555

1

Written by Debra Morris.

Illustration by Charlotte Smith Art and Illustration.

Design by Greg Wall.

THE REAL WORLD CUP

ONE TEAM ONE DREAM

by

Debra Morris

I feel every child, no matter what creed, colour, gender or ability deserves a feel-good story, where they see themselves in a book portraying how, with love, friendship and determination dreams really can come true.

The Real-World Cup, One Team, One Dream, is a story loosely based on children known to me and the global phenomenon that is FOOTBALL. I believe there is no greater platform to express the diversity of the human race than in sport and how easy it is to start a conversation and make new friends if you have just one thing in common.

CONTENTS

CHAPTER ONE

THE SINCLAIRS

"Kam, get in here this minute and tidy your room it's an absolute disgrace!" called Mum.

"Aww!! You've got to be joking mum. If I am going to be the best footballer in the world it's practice, practice, practice you know!" replied Kam.

Mum gave him that look, 'the' 'I won't ask you again look '. "You're eleven years old, you've got plenty of time to practice, even footballers need to keep their room tidy, no wonder half of your football socks are missing, I'll bet half of them are under your bed, if you kept it tidy, you'd have more time to practice".

"Why are mums so bossy, doesn't she realise who I am? 'King Kam' that's who, I'll be King of the World one day" he muttered to himself.

Kam ran upstairs trying not to waste any of his precious training time and tidied his room. Well, he pushed everything under his bed out of sight, then sat reading his football books until he thought enough time had passed that his mum would believe he had done a proper job. "Finished Mum, can I carry on training now?" he bellowed. He heard footsteps on the stairs.

"Ok, I'm coming up to check." called mum.

"All finished," said Kam as he hid his books under the duvet. "Wow, well I'm impressed, well done!" exclaimed mum, "You can stay out an extra hour to practice for doing such a good job!"

A huge grin appeared on Kam's face as he shouted, "Yes! more football!" He ran downstairs and back into the rear garden, he ran towards the ball, he flicked it up with his right foot, onto his left foot, flicked it back over his head turned and volleyed it straight into the back fence, Mum smiled to herself 'Hmm' she thought as she watched him from the bedroom window, '"I think he may be right, he could be the best in the world one day, the boy's obsessed, and talented, must take after me," she chuckled to herself.

At eleven years old, Kamron St. Clair, a boy of mixed heritage, his father Jamaican and his mother mixed English/Jamaican, is tall for his age and so appeared older than his years, except for his baby-faced features, big hazel eyes and long curly eyelashes, a wide smile, with a few gaps in his teeth where his baby teeth have fallen out and brown curly hair, long spirals on top that make him appear even taller. He lives with his mum Katie, a nurse at the local hospital, and his two brothers fourteen-year-old Diego and nine-year-old Ethan.

Diego is a tall and athletically built teenager, he has deep dark brown eyes, a perfect bright wide smile, and short dreadlocks. He takes so much pride in his hair each morning mum often asks if he's got a girlfriend as he won't leave the house unless it's just perfect.

A quiet but very studious boy, music and basketball is his passion and he spends a lot of his time after school either at basketball practice or producing music at music club and on his home computer with his best friend Ano, much to the rest of the family's delight, not!, the noise sometimes is unbearable, almost as unbearable as him tapping on everything no matter what he's doing, like his desk when he's doing his homework, tapping on the kitchen table during meal times, and most annoying of all tapping on the sofa when Kam and Ethan are trying to watch the match on T.V. Diego boasts he's going to become a music producer or a professional basket player when he's older, mum thinks he should concentrate more on his studies, but that's just what a mum would say isn't it?

Now, Ethan, he's just like his mum, he has her blue-green eyes, light brown curly hair, and a very cheeky smile. Ethan likes to do everything Kam likes to do with no exception, which didn't please Kam very much at all, he thinks he's a pest, a nuisance and a general pain in the butt at times and he follows Kam everywhere, much to Kam's annoyance, especially when it comes to his football, but Kam had already decided, nothing or anyone was going to get in the way of that.

CHAPTER TWO

THE BIG MAN NEXT DOOR

"Morning Dave!" shouted Kam, "Is training still on tomorrow?"

"Of course, Kam!" came a big bellowing voice from the garden next door.

Dave has been Kam's football coach for the last seven years and eventually his manager when he signed his first contract with Well Borne All Stars FC under 6's. Dave is a big, burly, very tall man, he has a kind face, a broad smile and a bigger than average afro. It's hilarious when Dave's in the back garden, all Kam sees is Dave's afro that appears to be walking along the fence all by itself, he finds it very entertaining but doesn't dare say anything for fear of upsetting his coach and being dropped to the subs bench for being cheeky.

When Kam was very young and he started to kick a ball about in his back garden, Dave got so fed up with the ball landing in his back garden on what seemed like every half an hour he thought to himself "that boy needs to learn how to control a football". So, he asked Kam's mum if she'd like to bring Kam for some football training once a week at the 'Well Bourne All Stars Academy', a local community football academy for kids that Dave runs with the help of a few of his old footballing friends, he thought Kam was a little young as he was still six months off his 5th birthday at the time, but he'd noticed how Kam only ever really played with the ball despite all the toys in the back garden and for a 4yr old he really did seem to have a passion for football and a few skills he'd learned watching the likes of Lionel Messi, Ronaldo, and Neymar Jr. on You Tube. His mum thought some training was a good idea too and so started taking Kam along on Monday evenings for a couple of hours.   Kam found it a little intimidating to begin with as everyone was a little older than him and the indoor sessions were very loud due to the acoustics of the domed roof at the academy, but Dave soon realised that Kam was a gifted little boy with natural ability for someone of his age and so once a week soon turned into three times a week. Kam made lots of new friends and his confidence and football skills improved immensely. Mum sometimes stayed to watch the training sessions, it gave Ethan some space to run around with a ball and pretend to be as good as his brother. Eventually, when he was old enough Ethan joined the training sessions too and showed he took after his big brother when it came to his footballing skills, he loved it, now Kam had someone at home to train with and they trained every day.

Secretly Dave was glad Katie came to watch her boys training, he'd thought how pretty she was the day she moved in next door with the boys, but for a big, confident man who was brilliant when it came to coaching noisy and sometimes disruptive kids, he was really quite a shy and reserved man, he'd often thought about asking Kam's mum and the boys round for tea, 'one day maybe' he thought I'll pluck up the courage.

CHAPTER THREE

THE GARAGE

The summer holidays had begun, the sun was shining, and everyone was outside in the garden, Diego was sitting on the patio with his laptop, and Kam and Ethan as usual were practicing their football skills and mum was cutting the lawn, the lawn with all the bald patches where the boys had worn it out playing football. Kam spotted the walking afro next door so climbed on to the bench next to the fence to see what Dave was up to.

"Morning Dave," said Kam.

"Morning Dave," said Ethan, what are you doing?

"Morning you two", "I'm tidying up my garage, I could do with some help if you're not too busy helping your mum," Kam thought for a moment, 'umm, raking up the grass and weeds when mum starts asking for some help or rummaging around in a garage full of old football stuff?' 'a bit of a no brainer' he thought,

'We'll help!' he said eagerly. "Mum, is it ok if we go round to help Dave clear out his garage, he said he needs some help?

"Please mum", said Ethan.

Mum looked at them "Well, I could do with some help later but I suppose it will keep you off the lawn so I can get it cut quicker, ok but make sure you're helping and not hindering him though" she said laughing.

"We're coming Dave," shouted Kam.

"We're coming round now Dave," shouted Ethan.

Kam looked at Ethan, lifted his eyes, why does he have

to copy everything I do? Mm, of course, I am King Kam that's why, he laughed to himself, he wants to be just like me.

Dave opened the side gate to let the boys in and Kam and Ethan walked towards the garage.

"Would you like a drink before we start boys?" Dave asked.

"Yes, please Dave" replied Kam.

"Yes, please Dave!" replied Ethan, predictably.

When they reached the garage they couldn't believe their eyes, there were boxes and boxes of stuff piled almost to the ceiling, old football kits, mangled football nets were strewn about, squashed footballs lying around, cones, corner flags, all sorts of stuff ...... Kam and Ethan looked at each other.

"Oh my, what a mess!!" they blurted out simultaneously, "Wish 'I'd stayed to help mum now" said Kam screwing up his face,

"Me too," said Ethan.

"I thought you'd say that" said Dave as he arrived with the drinks "have you changed your minds then?"

Kam looked up at Dave, he saw a sadness he hadn't seen in Dave before, Dave always seemed so happy and full of fun. "It's ok" said Kam, "it looks like you need us more than mum does right now,"

"Yeah Dave, we'll have this sorted in no time at all" said Ethan trying to sound positive but secretly thinking 'what have I let myself in for?'

Dave nodded, "Come on then, sooner we get this over with the sooner we can have a kick about."

"Ok boss!" said Kam, giving Dave a high five.

"We make a good team don't you think?"

"Yeah, like Bergkamp and Henry," said Dave. "

"Who?" Kam looked puzzled?"

York and Cole?"

"Who?" Kam frowned.

"Never mind," said Dave with a smile, "I must be getting old".

They started by pulling as much as they could out of the garage and placing everything in separate piles on the lawn. Kam grabbed the mangled nets, they were covered in dirt, dust, dried mud, and grass, oh and dead spiders and creepy crawlies, they'd obviously not been used for a very long time, Kam pulled and pulled, he used all his strength, but the nets wouldn't budge.

"Here let us give you a hand," said Dave, "It's stuck under this box, I'll lift it and you pull", "you ready?"

Kam took hold of the nets again, "Yes boss! I'm ready"

"On three" "One.... two.... three!"

Dave lifted the box, Kam pulled with all his might, he soon wished he hadn't pulled so hard, he stumbled backward, taking the nets with him, he fell to the ground, the nets on top of him. Kam's first thought was of all the spiders and creepy crawlies, and he began to panic, the more he struggled to get them off the more he got tangled in the dirty, smelly, critter infested nets.

"Arrrgh!!" get em off!! get em off!!"

Dave could hardly contain himself, his laugh got louder and louder.

"Stop struggling!"

But the more he struggled the more tangled Kam became, "Help me, somebody!"

Dave began to pull at the nets but because he was laughing so much, he became tangled too.

Ethan just stood there laughing. "Mum! Mum! come quickly" "You have got to see this!"

Mum and Diego ran over, climbed on to the bench next to the fence and peered over.

"How on Earth did that happen?" said mum laughing hysterically, hardly able to get her words out.

Dave and Kam were well and truly tangled, they stopped struggling, sat up and just looked at each other.

Dave shrugged his shoulders, "What do we do now buddy?"

A big grin appeared on Kam's face, and they laughed and laughed.

"Hold on I'm coming over" shouted Diego as he climbed

over the fence, "Pass me your garden shears, mum!"

Diego took the shears and carefully chopped at the nets until they fell away.

"Well, I wasn't looking forward to this job today, but you've made my day," said Dave still chuckling, "I'll go get us another drink boys, thirsty work this, Katie, would you like to come round for a drink too? you must be thirsty after all that gardening in this heat?"

"I'd love to" mum replied, blushing slightly.

Dave gave a little smile.

"But I'll walk around to the gate, you won't catch me climbing over any fences," she laughed.

Kam smiled to himself, my mum and Dave, I wonder, now that would be a great team too, he thought.

Dave brought the tray of drinks outside and placed them on the table shaded beneath the big oak tree at the bottom of the garden.

"Over here boys, come and get it!"

The ice-cold drinks were a welcome break, it was a hot day and there wasn't much shade in the garden apart from the huge tree, Ethan being Ethan ran and sat down first and picked up the glass with the most juice in it, "Where's the snacks then?" he asked.

"Don't be cheeky!" said mum looking a little embarrassed, "It's ok" said Dave laughing, "I've heard how Ethan likes his food and there's nothing wrong with having a healthy appetite, is there mate?" "Come on then, let's see what I've got in the kitchen".

"You don't have to ask me twice," laughed Ethan as he jumped up and followed Dave into the house. Ten minutes later they came back with a tray of Jamaican bun and cheese, a bowl of crisps and another large jug of iced orange juice. Everyone sat around eating and chatting until the sun began to go down.

"Right, I think I need to get you three home now, you can help me put the mower and garden tools away before you get showered, it's been a long day, and a very funny one, thanks for the entertainment today Dave, I've not laughed so much in ages."

"You're welcome" Dave replied, "I've really enjoyed myself too, and if the boys aren't busy tomorrow we can carry on where we left off."

"Ok see you tomorrow boss" shouted Kam as he made his way through the gate.

"Me too," shouted Ethan.

"Fine by me," replied Mum, "see you tomorrow then, and thanks again for a fun afternoon, it was lovely, it really was."

CHAPTER FOUR

THE TEAM TALK

The next morning was as bright and sunny as the previous day, Kam was first downstairs and helped himself to breakfast, then came Ethan, followed by Mum and Diego, they all sat down at the table together, it made a nice change to sit, and chat compared to the usual chaotic mornings on a typical school day where everyone is rushing to get out the door on time.

"So, what's the plan for today?" said Mum, "What do you fancy doing?"

"Well, we did promise to help Dave today, we didn't get much done yesterday, did we?" replied Kam "And he really does need our help with that pile of junk in his garage."

"Ok, well I think I'll just make the most of a ball free garden, I'll get the sun lounger out and relax for a change." Mum said rubbing her hands together, "Today's sounding like a good day already".

Diego piped up "Well I'm expecting Ano any minute now, his parents have got to work, and he doesn't fancy spending the whole day with his bossy sister."

"Ok that's fine" replied Mum "But I don't want you sitting inside at the computer playing games all day, you need to find something else to do."

The door knocked and there, right on time, was Ano. "Come in Ano" gestured Diego, "We're just having breakfast".

"Morning everyone!" he called in his usual happy smiley tone.

"Morning Ano, would you like breakfast with us?" asked Kam.

"Well, I've already had breakfast but I wouldn't say no to seconds" he said rubbing his stomach.

"Well, take a seat and help yourself Ano" said Diego reaching for a fresh bowl.

"Oh, thank you, and we'll clear the table and wash up if you like Ms. St. Clair, "Won't we Diego?"

"Aww thank you Ano, I'm sure Diego was about to offer anyway," said Mum smiling, "That's very kind of you." Diego shook his head and squirmed at Ano.

"Ha! thanks Ano," said Kam laughing.

"It's ok Kam, it's your turn tomorrow," laughed mum. "Aww, why can't we just get a dishwasher," asked Kam.

Mum laughed, "Right I'll leave you two to clear up then." "Actually Diego" smiled Ano, "I've been thinking, shall we help Dave clear his garage too, it could be fun, besides, he's always helping other people, so he deserves a helping hand occasionally don't you think?

"You're a kind boy Ano" smiled mum, "I think he'd really appreciate that".

Diego wasn't as impressed. "You and your bright ideas Ano, I suppose I've got no choice now, this is a once in a lifetime opportunity for you to see me doing any kind of manual labour so make the most of it" he laughed.

Diego and Ano cleared the table, washed up and then the four boys walked next door and knocked on Dave's door. "Morning boys, smiled Dave, you're nice and early" he was surprised to see Diego and Ano but glad of the extra helping hands. "Come on through boys, would you like a drink before we get started?"

"Yes please," they all replied".

"What about you Kam? Kam?" called Dave.

But Kam didn't reply,

"Where's that boy got to?" asked Dave curiously.

As he was passing Dave's desk in the hallway a poster on top of a pile of paperwork had caught Kam's eye.

"What's this Dave? are we going to the World Cup Final?" "What do you mean?" asked Dave.

"This poster, it says 'Win tickets to the World Cup Final'. "Oh that? blimey, you've got eyes like a hawk, that my son is a football tournament and a very tough one at that, there are teams from all around the world competing, the winning team gets to attend the World Cup Final at Wembley Stadium this summer, they'll get to meet the best players in the world and be given the best seats in the house".

Dave smiled; he knew what was coming next.

"Wow! that sounds amazing," said Kam, "Do you think we could enter?"

"Well, you need good players, really good players and lots of luck to win a worldwide competition like that. "We've got some great players at the academy that could compete at that level", Kam puffed out his chest and smiled, "Yes Kam that includes you, but we've not got enough really good players to create a team capable at competing at that level".

"Oh, please Dave", pleaded Ethan "What have we got to lose? seriously, if we don't win at, least we'll have taken part, it's a fantastic opportunity for kids like us, we'd get some experience at playing against world-class players, learn some new skills, maybe teach them a few things too."

Dave butted in "Ok, Ok I get the picture, I'll give it some thought," not knowing whether to be impressed by the boy's enthusiasm and confidence or dread telling them the academy almost certainly didn't have the funds required to enter such a big competition. The academy depends on the goodwill of the coaches giving up their free time to help the kids in the local community. Dave didn't know how he was going to get the boys to the World Cup, but nothing was going to stop him trying.

CHAPTER FIVE

DAVE

"Right let's get on with the job in hand, I've made a start already but that garage is in a right old mess so I'm really grateful to you boys, I've not been in there for years, who knows what we're going to find, I dread to think," Dave said grimacing, "And I hate creepy crawlies so if you see any be sure to let me know, I can't stand the little critters."

"Don't be scared Dave, they won't hurt you!" laughed Kam.

They began by dragging as much as they could out onto the lawn, sorting out anything worth keeping, most of which were compiled of cones, a few brand-new balls of various sizes that just needed inflating, boxes of bibs, tracksuit tops, and water bottles. They piled up the rest to be taken to the local tip.

"Right, you lot carry on, I'll go get us some refreshments, thirsty work this" puffed Dave," I'll be back in five."

"Right oh gaffa!" shouted Ethan, using his top to wipe the sweat from his forehead, I'll have ice in mine too please."

"Right ok!" Dave shouted as he entered the kitchen.

Right at the back of the garage, there was what looked like an old metal locker. It was partly covered with a large piece of tarpaulin which the boys managed to drag off without pulling the locker over.

"Wonder what's in there," said Ano.

"Only one way to find out," said Kam, "Open it".

Kam turned the handle, but it wouldn't budge.

"Let me try" insisted Ethan.

"This calls for a bit more muscle than you've got " laughed Diego, "Out of my way you weaklings!"

Diego grabbed hold of the handle and pulled down on it with all his might, gritting his teeth, but it wouldn't budge.

"I Think you might need this!" The boys turned round to find Ethan stood with a smirk on his face, holding a key he'd spotted on the floor. "Told you to let me have a go, didn't I?"

Ethan walked over to the cabinet and inserted the key, slowly turning it....... Ta-da!

"There you go boys" he laughed as the locker opened.

"Wow look at all those trophies! They're Dave's from when he was a kid" exclaimed Kam "I bet he's forgotten they were in here" "Hey Dave, look what we've found in that old locker at the back of the garage."

Dave walked towards them with the drinks.

"What have you got there then?" he asked.

"How come you've never told us how good you used to be?" asked Kam.

"What are you talking about?" asked Dave.

"We've found all these old football trophies with your name on them in the back of the garage, in that cupboard, there are loads of them, you must have been *really* good" said Ano.

"Oh those old things" replied Dave "Yes I was pretty good" he laughed, "And if you keep training every day maybe you'll be as good as I was one day."

"Yeah, yeah" laughed Kam, remember this name 'King Kam' I'm going to be the best in the world one day, you'll see!"

"Who are these people in these photo's Dave?" called Ethan, "Is this your family?"

Kam noticed that same sad look on Dave's face again. "What's wrong Dave? are you ok?" he asked.

"I'm ok lads, really".

"Why do you look so sad then?" asked Ethan.

"Ethan, can't you see he's upset? just leave it," said Kam.

"Sorry Dave," said Ethan, "But you always tell us talking is the best medicine when you're sad or upset".

"Yes, I do, don't I? Ok boys let's take a break, bring your drinks and I'll tell you all about it."

They all sat down under the big tree where it was much cooler and Dave picked up the photographs, cleared his throat, took a deep breath, and began to tell his story.

"This man here is my father 'Ranako', the name means 'handsome' where my father was born, a village called Migos in Nigeria, West Africa, I think I take after my father actually, he is a handsome man don't you think," Dave smiled.

The boys looked at each other and burst out laughing.

"Well, mum thinks so," said Ethan, "I heard her say she thought you were good looking when she was on the telephone to her friend the other day. She told me not to tell you when she realised, I'd overheard her, so don't tell her I told you" He laughed.

Dave looked at Ethan and smiled, "Well that's good to know" smiled Dave trying not to blush, "And I think your mum is very pretty too," smiled Dave.

"Anyway, let's continue, this is my mother 'Ife' it means 'love' in Africa, and she has lots of love to give everyone. This picture here is of myself and my twin brother 'Ade', we would be around 2 years old in this picture, it was taken just before he became ill with a fever, he needed to see a doctor but the nearest hospital was very far away, mum and dad agreed that my father would go with him and my mother would stay home to look after me, so off they went, when they reached the hospital it was clear that my brother was really poorly, the doctors said my brother would need to stay in hospital for around two weeks before he would be well enough to go home.

After a few days, my father had to return home to work but the nurses said my brother would be well looked after and that my father should return in two weeks to collect him. That would be the last time we were to see my brother. When my father returned to collect him, my brother was nowhere to be found. To this day we have no idea what happened to him, maybe one day I'll find out," he said with tears in his eyes. For once the boys were silent, looking at each other not knowing what to say, not even Ethan and he always had something to say.

Dave continued "My parents were heartbroken, they searched for him high and low, but no one seemed to know what had happened to him and so when I was four years old, my father, who was a teacher was offered a job in England. My mother was so sad to leave but it was also a constant reminder of my lost brother and so they agreed to move to England for my mother to be near her sister who had moved here a few years before. We moved to Well Bourne and the rest, as they say, is history.

I played football for a local team in my youth before turning professional, unfortunately, I got injured which meant I had to give up my dream and so I turned to coaching. Which is how I ended up coaching you ugly lot!"

That remark broke the ice and the boys laughed out loud, "Hey, less of the ugly" said Kam screwing up his face.

Dave stood up, "Right, drink up we've got work to do!"

The boys went back to the garage whilst Dave began filling the skip with all the old training stuff.

CHAPTER SIX

THE MAGIC BEGINS

Diego and Ano were rifling through the boxes of training kits, the socks, shorts, tops, and bibs were being separated into individual boxes, Ethan was stacking cones as high as he could reach, and Kam was sorting the boxes of footballs into separate boxes depending on their size. When he had almost reached the bottom of the second box, he noticed a brightly coloured piece of cloth poking out from underneath the footballs.

"I wonder what that is? he wondered, only one way to find out." He pushed the deflated balls to one side to reveal the brightly coloured cloth, it was covered in bright pink flowers with purple leaves, orange and brown diamond shapes surrounded the flowers and the cloth was edged in red and blue zig-zag lines.

"Wow! This looks like it's from Africa!"

He lifted the cloth out of the box and placed it on the floor in front of him. Opening the cloth up gently to reveal a box, and inside the box was a fully inflated leather football made up of the same colours and pattern as the cloth it had been wrapped in.

"Wow! look at this! I've never seen a football like this before!" exclaimed Kam.

Kam, Diego, Ano, and Ethan gathered around the ball.

"That just doesn't make sense, it must have been in there for years, how come it's still inflated?" said Diego frowning.

"That looks like African art," said Ano, "My dad's got some shirts like that, he wears them in the summer."

38

"You wouldn't catch me wearing something like that!" laughed Ethan.

"Well, you would if you lived in Africa Ethan," replied Ano, "It's what everyone wears, people wear bright colours because it's very hot there."

Diego interrupted "Every country has their own way of dressing Ethan; it would be a bit boring if everyone around the world dressed the same, wouldn't it? Imagine everyone in onesies like that big penguin one you've got," he laughed.

"I suppose so," squirmed Ethan, "It just looks weird that's all, but as Will.I.Am would say, we've only got one world, one world" Ethan started singing in his best American accent.

"There you go then," said Kam "We're all different, and the same, one world, we've only got one world!"

Kam brought the ball out into the garden and called out to Dave.

"Was this your ball when you were a kid in Africa Dave?" he asked. "Here, catch!" called Kam, as he threw the ball to him.

"Where did you find that Kam?" asked Dave.

"In that box over there, it was wrapped in this!" replied Kam.

"I've never seen it before in my life, but it certainly looks like some sort of African art to me. How did you inflate it? I can't see anywhere to insert a pump." asked Dave.

"That's how I found it, fully inflated," said Kam.

"How strange," Dave replied, scratching his head. He tossed the ball over to Kam, Kam caught it on his left foot, flicked it onto his right foot, then turned and backheeled it back to Dave hitting him in the chest.

"Show off! Is that all you've got?" He laughed as he threw it back at Kam. Kam chested the ball down onto his right foot and Kam began to play keepy-uppy, he kicked it high into the air and was watching it fall as he said,

"Can I take it home?" The ball landed on his right foot just as he said the word 'home' and 'THE WEIRDEST THING HAPPENED!!' Kam looked around and he was standing in the middle of his back garden, Dave, Diego, Ano, and Ethan were all peering over the fence, speechless!

"Whoa! Whoa! what happened?" spluttered Kam.

He stood motionless staring at the ball.

"What is that ...thing?" he said nervously."

"Kam! Kam! Diego called out, "Kick the ball again and this time say, 'next door', and see if it transports you back here."

Kam reluctantly picked up the ball, not wanting to appear scared in front of the others. He threw the ball into the air, watched it falling again and just as it hit his left shouted, "Next door!" WHOOSH!! Kam looked around at his surroundings, again he'd been transported, but this time he was in the opposite neighbour's garden. He could hear Dave and the others laughing uncontrollably. Kam quickly picked up the ball in case grumpy Mr. Smith, Kam's other next-door neighbour, came out to see what was going on with all the noise they were making. He threw the ball into the air once more and as it hit his left foot called out "Dave's garden!"

True to form Kam had indeed been transported back into Dave's back garden.

"WOW! That ball is something special" exclaimed Diego excitedly. Ano just stood open-mouthed unable to speak.

"Wow! just Wow!" said Ethan.

Kam picked up the ball and walked over to them all. Dave took the ball from him.

"Not a word to anyone about this," Dave whispered putting his finger to his lips, "It's special! It's here for a reason and we're going to find out exactly what that reason is!".

"Reason for what?"

The boys laughed as Dave almost jumped out of his skin.

"Oh, Hi Katie" he replied looking rather sheepish, he looked back at the boys "I think we need a team meeting right now don't you think?"

"Yes, I think 'WE' do!" said mum, Mum walked over to the seating area beneath the big tree and sat down.

"Ok, come on boys, sit! and tell me all about it." and

that's exactly what they did.

CHAPTER SEVEN

THE PLAN

Next morning Kam came down for breakfast, Mum was sitting at the kitchen table with her usual morning coffee. "Morning Mum, you look nice today, how come you've done your hair and makeup already? Asked Kam, "Are you going somewhere nice?"

"Do you fancy pancakes this morning Kam? I know they're your favourite".

Kam looked at mum half smiling, half frowning, "Love some!" he replied licking his lips, "What have I done to deserve this?"

"I'm in a good mood" mum replied.

"Why's that then? You hoping to see Dave today? Is that why you look so nice this morning?" he grinned.

Mum blushed "What are you talking about?"

"Oh, nothing" he smiled, "just asking that's all".

"Do you want these pancakes making or not?" she said smiling.

"Yes please!" I think Diego and Ethan will be down in a minute so might as well make a few," he winked. At that Diego and Ethan appeared at the door.

"Did someone mention pancakes?" they said simultaneously.

"You've got ears bigger than your tummies you two!" she laughed, "Come, and sit down they'll be ready in a jiffy."

Just as they began to eat there was a knock at the front

door.

"I'll get it," said Mum

"Morning Dave, what brings you here so early?"

"Morning Katie, sorry if I've interrupted breakfast but I need to talk to you and the boys if that's ok?" he replied.

"Of course, replied mum, "Come in, would you like a coffee? We're having pancakes too if you fancy them?"

"That would be lovely thanks Katie," Dave replied.

Kam looked up at Mum and smiled.

"So, what's up boss?" asked Ethan.

"Well, when I've finished these delicious pancakes, we need to have a serious conversation about an idea I have." he winked looking over at Kam.

As soon as they'd finished eating, they all gathered around the table and Dave began.

"Remember that football competition you were asking about the other day? Well, I've got an idea of how we can find new players to add to our team."

Kam punched the air "Yes!", "we're going to the World Cup!"

"Hey! calm down, I'm not saying we will win the competition but we're certainly going to give it our best shot," chuckled Dave, "I love your confidence though, you're going to need that son".

"Right! here's the plan," Everyone leaned in so as not to miss a thing.

"That ball we found in my garage yesterday, I think we could use it to help us find new players."

"How is it going to do that?" asked Kam.

"Well, if that ball is as magic as I think it is, it's going to take us around the world to find new players, but not just any new players, the best players!"

"Wow! That's brilliant!" exclaimed Kam.

"Hang on a minute," said Mum nervously, "How do you know it will work? and most of all how do you know it's going to be safe?"

Dave took a deep breath....... "Well, I don't, and that's why I'm going to try it out this afternoon."

Mum gasped, clutching her face with both hands, she looked over at Kam, "Don't even think about it!" said Mum sternly.

"I didn't say anything, but I was going to ask to go with him though," Kam laughed.

"I need to try it out first Kam," said Dave "if all goes well then the world's our oyster."

"Aren't you scared Dave?" asked Ethan, "It sounds dangerous to me."

"Of course, I'm a little scared, but I'm going to give it a go so wish me luck, meet me next door at 2 o'clock this afternoon."

Dave stood up, "I've got a really good feeling about this so don't worry, I'll be fine."

The morning passed quickly.

"Mum, are you coming round to Dave's house, it's nearly 2 o'clock?" asked Ethan.

"Don't worry Dave knows what he's doing...I think...I hope," said Ethan nervously.

"I'm ready," said Mum, "Well as ready as I'll ever be, I just hope he's going to be ok; I've got used to having Dave around, I'd hate for something to happen to him."

Kam nudged Diego, "Told you she liked him,"

Diego smiled, "I've got used to having him around too actually, he's a top man, and Mum deserves the best, maybe we should invite him round for dinner when he gets back." he whispered.

Kam gave Diego a high-five, "Good idea," winked Kam. "What are you two up to?" frowned Mum, "Come on before Dave thinks we've abandoned him."

When they arrived next door, Dave appeared nervous, but also excited at the same time.

"I was beginning to think you weren't coming,"

"Wouldn't miss today for anything," replied Kam excitedly "Not even football?" asked Dave.

"Not today, not even football," laughed Kam.

Everyone walked out into the back garden, Dave

unlocked the garage and Kam ran inside to get the ball, he'd hidden it, in a box within a box, under a pile of Astroturf right at the back of the garage. "Got it!" he shouted.

Dave took the ball from him, and they all gathered below the big oak tree. "Right, let's see what this ball can actually do!"

Mum looked nervous "Be careful Dave, make sure you come back to us!"

Dave lifted the ball ready to drop it onto his right foot. "I'll try somewhere nearby first just in case," he laughed nervously. "Ok, here goes!" He took a deep breath and dropped the ball, as it hit his right foot he called out "Well Bourne Academy!"........everyone gasped......and waited, but nothing happened, "Maybe that's too far," Dave said disappointedly.

"Try again!" called out Diego.

"Ok, here goes again," said Dave picking up the ball, he took another deep breath and dropped the ball to his right foot "Well Bourne Academy!" again nothing happened.

"Aww!" moaned Kam, we didn't imagine what happened yesterday, what's wrong with it? Stupid thing!" he sobbed, he picked up the ball, throwing it into the air, just as it was about to hit the floor Kam kicked it away, "Might as well go home!" As if by magic Kam disappeared. Kam had been transported next door, he was standing in his kitchen, just like the day before the ball had followed his instruction.

"Kam! Kam!" He could hear Mum calling; Kam ran out into the back garden.

"I'm here Mum! Stop stressing I'm fine!", He picked up the ball and kicked it again calling out "Dave's garden!" Whoosh! and there he was, back in Dave's garden with the biggest grin on his face, looking rather pleased with himself. "Oh my Gosh!" exclaimed Mum, "It really is magic," Dave and the boys just stood staring at her, it was then the awful realisation dawned, it was Kam the ball performed for.

"I don't like the idea of this."

"It'll be fine Mum." Laughed Kam excitedly.

"No! absolutely not!" snapped Mum, "No way!"

"Right let's all calm down," said Dave, "Kam's not going anywhere with that ball unless I go with him, how about we try it together?"

Dave and Kam linked arms, "Ok! try again Kam."

Kam threw the ball into the air once more and called out "Well Borne Academy!" Whoosh! Whoosh!! and they were gone, Dave and Kam were now standing in the middle of the gym at the academy. Kam punched the air and began to 'floss', Dave burst out laughing and joined in.

"Right, we need to calm down and get back before your mum starts panicking, are you ready Kam?"

"Yes, boss!" Kam laughed, he could hardly contain his excitement, linking arms again, Kam threw the ball up

and as it hit his left foot called out "Dave's garden!"
Whoosh! Whoosh! True to form, the ball transported
them back to Dave's garden where Mum, Diego, and
Ethan were waiting nervously for their return.   Mum
ran over and hugged Kam, "Are you, ok son?"

"Of course, I am, you're such a stress-head" he laughed
through his squished-up face, but you're crushing me, I
can't breathe!"

"Oops! sorry! Mum laughed, "It's only because I love
you!"

"Ok! Mum, don't embarrass me any further, you'll ruin
my street cred."

"Right! How about I make us all lunch?" said Mum, "Link
arms! Are you ready Kam?", they all linked arms, Kam
kicked the ball and called out "Home!" .... Whoosh!
Whoosh!! and they were all back at No.62.

"Yay!" does that mean we can start making plans for the
team then Mum?" asked Kam excitedly.

"Of course, so long as we can do it together, I don't see
why not." Mum replied.

"Thanks, Katie," said Dave "It's going to be great, you'll
see, but I think I'd better keep this ball at my house, not
that I don't trust you, Kam," he laughed.

Kam screwed up his face and laughed. "Probably for the
best I suppose."

That afternoon they all sat down at the kitchen table
discussing their plans for the 'best team in the world' to

compete in the upcoming World Cup tournament. Dave decided they'd need at least ten new players including substitutes, Kam made a list of the positions they needed to fill and mum, and Diego went through what kit would be required. Ethan typically thought of his tummy and made a list of what food he'd like to take with him. Tomorrow would be the day the big adventure would really start, and Kam's dream would really begin to come true, he looked up at the ceiling 'King Kam!" that's who I am he thought to himself, "I can't wait!'

CHAPTER EIGHT

THE SEARCH

Mum drew the curtains back, squinting as the sun burst into the room, she pushed open the bedroom window and the sound of birdsong came flooding in, "mm! it looks like a good day for a good day", she thought. It was only just after 6 am but she wanted to get an early start preparing for the big adventure ahead, she needed time to think without the constant noise of the boys, she knew they'd be even noisier today with all the excitement ahead. Then she heard, "Morning Mum!", with raised eyebrows mum turned round to see Kam, already in his football gear at the bedroom door, she smiled,

"I can't get a minute's peace around here, can I?"

"Love you too Mum", laughed Kam as he blew her a kiss.

Mum entered the ensuite in her room only to find the shower already running and steamed up,

"Big Dave, there's only one big Dave, there's only one big Dave!" Ethan had beaten her to it.

"Ethan how come you're up so early and who said you could use my shower?", Mum called out a little annoyed.

"Morning Mum, Kam was using the other one, I didn't think you'd mind, I couldn't sleep, I'm just too excited for today," he replied.

"And what's that you're singing about Dave?", Mum asked.

"Oh! were you impressed", laughed Ethan, "It just

came to me as I was enjoying the shower, he's big and he's named Dave and I think he's great, we're so lucky he's our friend, there really is only one big Dave like him".

"Well, I can't disagree with that", replied Mum smiling to herself, "Now hurry up, we've got a big day ahead of us". "Right oh!" spluttered Ethan, "I'll be done in a jiffy".

As they all sat down for breakfast there was a knock at the door. Diego jumped up, at the door was Ano and his dad, Diego high-fived Ano, "Morning Mr. Abara",

"Morning everyone, it is a beautiful day today!" Mr Abara replied, "I hope you are all well. Ano has been telling me all about your plans to create a football team for this year's Youth World Cup tournament, I would like to help you if I may." Mum made the visitors a drink and they all gathered around the kitchen table to listen to what Ano's dad had to say.

Ano's dad began, " I was born in a wonderful place called Migos in Nigeria, West Africa."

"Oh my gosh!" blurted Kam, "that's where Dave was born".

"Well," continued Mr. Abara, "My brother Bako still lives there, he is the headteacher at the school on the edge of the village. The children come from far and wide each day to attend their classes. It is a happy place, filled with love and laughter, my brother is very proud of his school, the teachers, and his pupils, and he says they have a pretty good football team.

A short while ago over the telephone he told me, that, last summer a man, a football coach, came to the village to scout for boys to join his football team in England, his name was Joseph Romenio, he and his coaches were so impressed with some of the boys footballing skills, they wanted to take the boys to England to join his youth football team, Chelski United. Have you heard of them?"

"Heard of them, they're the best team in England!" Kam gasped.

"Oh! sorry Kam," Mr. Abara replied, "I don't follow football so I wouldn't know about these kinds of things."

"So how many boys came to England then?" asked Kam. "None of them," Mr. Abara replied, "The parents of the boys could not afford to travel to England with their children, so the boys weren't allowed to go."

"Wow!" exclaimed Ethan, "Those boys must be really good or Romenio would not have wanted to sign them up."

"Exactly," said Kam excitedly, "We need to tell Dave, I think we may have just found ourselves some new players! Wait here everyone, I'll go and get Dave, he needs to hear this."

Kam hurried round to Dave's house, banging loudly on the front door,

"Dave! Dave!"

"Hey Kam, what's up? Calm down, what's the matter?"

Kam took a deep breath and repeated what Mr. Abara had just told them. Dave didn't say a word, he followed Kam back to no.62 and into the kitchen where everyone was waiting, Dave looked around the room, took a deep breath and said,

"Well boys, Katie, it looks like we're going to Africa!"

The whole room erupted, "YAY!!" The boys were jumping up and down high fiving each other.

Dave noticed Mum looking a little unsure, he put a reassuring arm around her shoulder, "Don't worry Katie, it'll be fine".

Dave shook Mr. Abara's hand, "Thank you Mr. Abara for offering to help".

"Please, call me Benedict, my friends call me Benedict". "I've got a good feeling about this Dave", you're a good man, we've been neighbours for many years, and I have nothing but admiration for you and what you do for this community, so thank you for all your hard work!"

"Thank you, Benedict, I've got a good feeling about this too".

Finally, everyone calmed down and they all sat around the kitchen table to put the plans in place for their BIG adventure. It was decided, at 10 o'clock on Wednesday morning, two days from now, it would be time for their journey to Migos, Nigeria, Africa!

CHAPTER NINE

WEDNESDAY

The big day arrived; Mum had spent the previous two days packing. The boys' clothes, training kits, trainers and football boots were all stacked up on the patio in huge holdalls, Mum had packed her stuff in what can only be described as the brightest, blingiest, yellow suitcase you'd ever seen, covered in pink flamingoes it really couldn't be any brighter.

"Whoa! Good job I've brought my sunglasses", Mum turned round to see Dave shielding his eyes from the suitcase.

"Ha, ha, very funny! at least it won't get mixed up with the rest of the stuff".

"Indeed!" laughed Dave.

Ano and his dad had arrived with their luggage, and everyone congregated in the back garden.

"Did you bring the ball, Dave?" asked Diego.

"How could I forget?" he replied "If everyone is ready, I think it's time we made our move."

Everyone made a circle around the luggage and Dave took the ball from his backpack and placed it at Kam's feet. "Right Kam!", "You know what to do, everyone link arms, and remember Kam, *Migos, Nigeria, Africa!*"

"Migos, Nigeria, Africa, Migos, Nigeria, Africa," Kam repeated to himself. Kam took two steps back, then took one step forward and thrust his left foot forward towards the ball, kicking it as hard as he could and shouted "Migos, Nigeria, Africa!".

Whoosh! Whoosh! ....In what seemed like a blink of an eye Kam shouted "Wow, open your eyes, everyone!" "We're here, we did it, we really did it!"

"Oh my gosh! It's so hot!" puffed Ethan removing his hoody.

"You're not kidding!" Diego replied, removing his cap to wipe the sweat from his forehead.

"Glad we wore our shorts", gasped Kam, "I'm sweating already".

"Mm! something smells good", laughed Ethan as he breathed in the cooking smells wafting around. "I can't wait for dinner!"

"Typical Ethan", laughed Dave.

Block built houses, some topped with corrugated iron, some topped with tiles, each one painted a different colour lined the dusty road, goats bleating, chickens squawking, children running around laughing and playing. Women in brightly coloured skirts, t-shirts, and headscarves were busying themselves, some had small babies strapped to their backs. Further up the hill, the sound of tools and machinery could be heard, some of the Migos men were building a new schoolhouse. Suddenly the villagers became aware of their visitors and they began to gather, staring, whispering to each other.

"Oh my, I'm home!" everyone looked around at Mr. Abara, wiping a tear from his eye.

"Why are you crying Dad?" asked Ano.

61

"They're happy tears son, I'm just so glad to be here, to see my family, it's been a long time since I saw them, they'll be so surprised and happy to meet you Ano, I haven't been back home since you were born".

Ano gave his dad a hug.

Suddenly a gap appeared amongst the villagers that had gathered,

"Well come and say hello!".

Mr. Abara looked up, to see a familiar figure.

"Bako! my brother it's so good to see you."

"Benedict, it is wonderful to see you!"

"What a surprise! You didn't tell me you were coming; how did you all get here? I didn't hear the bus arrive." Grinning, Mr. Abara looked over at Dave and the boys, "Well it's a bit of an adventure, a long story, I'll tell you all about it later", he smiled. "Let me introduce you to my friends, this is my neighbour Dave, the football coach",

Dave and Bako shook hands, "And here we have the lovely Katie", Bako took hold of Katie's hand gently kissing the back of it,

"Lovely to meet you, Katie," smiled Bako

"Say hello to Katies' sons Diego, Kam, and Ethan", the boys each shook Bako's hand, "And finally, this is my son Ano who's been wanting to meet you all for such a long time".

"Finally, I meet my nephew, my what a handsome boy you are, welcome, everyone! I am so happy to meet you all, come, you must stay with us, my family will be so happy to meet you and you can tell me all about this adventure of yours while we eat".

Ethan licked his lips "sounds good to me," he laughed rubbing his stomach.

As they made their way to Bako's house the boys took in the sights, the sounds, and the smells of the village. It appeared a busy but happy place. Small village shops adorned the route, handmade jewelry stores, a barber, food stores, clothing and woven cloth stores, Dave spotted Katie eyeing up the jewelry as they walked by and smiled to himself, some of the villagers came out of their houses to greet the visitors as they passed, and children began to follow them, giggling and laughing but excited to meet some new friends.

As they reached the edge of the village, they arrived at a two-story house built from white painted blocks, topped off with a corrugated roof. A row of three large windows lined up across the first floor and the on the ground floor a wooden front door painted bright orange sat in the middle of two further windows. Each window had shutters to keep out the searing heat and the front garden consisted of a vegetable patch and large plants with enormous leaves.

"Here we are, this is my house, please come in and make yourselves at home", said Bako as he bowed and waved the visitors up the steps and onto the front porch.

Bako's wife greeted them at the door, "Welcome everyone, what a wonderful surprise, please come in".

"Let me introduce you to my wife Nala", said Bako, summoning everyone inside. Leaving the bags on the porch they entered the house, it felt much cooler inside, mainly because of the ceiling fans, the bare wooden floorboards and the breeze blowing through the open windows. The wooden furniture was basic but expertly crafted and family pictures adorned the walls alongside handwoven rugs. After the introductions, Nala bought fresh homemade lemonade from the kitchen, and everyone sat around chatting and getting to know each other.

"Dave!"

" Yes, Kam?"

"Do you think we could have a couple of footballs so we can have a kick about outside?"

"Sure, why not Kam? It will give us a chance to unpack and get settled in peace and give you boys the chance to introduce yourselves to the local kids. You never know you may find the next Lionel Messi amongst them," he laughed.

"Well, that's why we're here Dave, to build our team, it's going to be amazing!" replied Kam grinning from ear to ear. Dave loosened the humongous drawstring bag and scooped out a couple of balls and threw them in Kam's direction, making sure the 'special' ball remained safely at the bottom of the bag.

"Cheers boss!" shouted Kam, "see you later, "

"Yeah!" shouted Ethan, "Just let us know when dinner is ready".

"You'll be the first to know Ethan", Dave laughed shaking his head.

Kam and Ethan hurried outside quickly followed by Diego and Ano. A group of boys who had been sitting on the porch opposite Bako's house came over to say hello.

"Hi, my name is Darnell, Darnell-Lessi and these are my friends, Marc-Bashford, Caetano-Donaldo, Samuel-Bronson, Pele-Ali and Arnold- Alexander"

Kam stood still for a moment, frowning, mm! he thought to himself, something sounds very familiar here but couldn't quite get his head around it, never mind he thought, let's just hope they can play football.

"Hello, my name is Kam, these are my brothers, Diego and Ethan and our friend Ano. We've travelled from England looking for players to join our World Cup team. Do you have somewhere we could play?"

"Sure," replied Darnell-Lessi, as he and the rest of the boys summoned them behind Bako's house.

Kam's eyes lit up as soon as they turned the corner, although rather dusty, there, right in front of him was a football pitch complete with line markings and rather rusty goalposts.

"Right let's see what you lot are made of", laughed Kam showing off his keepy-uppy skills.

Darnell-Lessi and his friends smiled at each other.

"Let's go, boys, I think these English boys are in for a bit of a surprise," winked Samuel.

Kam threw them a ball.........it never even touched the ground, Darnell-Lessi and his friends passed the ball between them, kicking it, heading it, knee tapping, overhead kicks...... Diego, Ano, and Ethan just stood watching, eyes wide like saucers in disbelief. Kam could not believe his eyes, "WOW! where did you learn to do that?" he exclaimed, the boys passed the ball back to him, Kam trapped the ball and just stood with his foot on top of it, hands-on-hips, staring in disbelief.

"You guys are AMAZING! Where did you learn all those skills? You must practice all the time."

"Well Darnell-Lessi's dad trains us, he's an amazing coach," replied Samuel, "We train here three times a week, then play matches on Saturdays or Sundays, we are training here tomorrow if you would like to join us?"

"Try and stop us," laughed Kam, "I can't wait to tell Dave about you guy's".

"Who is Dave?" asked Pele-Ali.

"He's our coach and he's amazing too, you'll get to meet him tomorrow, he's not going to want to miss this training session for the world when I tell him how good you are." The boys carried on with their kick about, showing off their individual ball skills, until they were summoned back to Bako's house, much to Ethan's delight as his tummy had begun making those ever-familiar grumbling noises.

"See you here at 6 o'clock tomorrow then boys?" shouted Arnold-Alexander.

"Definitely!" replied Kam with the biggest smile on his face, "Tomorrow can't come soon enough!"

The boys' fist pumped each other as they left the pitch and went their separate ways, all of them excited to meet up again, and Ethan eager to get back to Bako's house for dinner ran all the way back.

Over dinner, the boys talked to Dave about their new friends. Dave could see how excited they all were, Kam especially, he looked around the table, everyone was chatting and laughing with each other, "This really is a special place," he thought to himself, "I can't remember living here as a child because I was so young, but I've been here less than a day and I feel so at home already." He looked over at Katie and realised how much she had come to mean to him, he knew he had come to love her and the boys but never had the confidence to tell her how he felt. "I think this is the right time and the right place to tell her how I feel, I must find the strength to tell her before we return to England."

CHAPTER TEN

TRAINING DAY

As Kam woke next morning and realised it hadn't all been just an amazing dream, he jumped out of bed and headed downstairs. He could hear cockerels crowing but not much else except Nala singing whilst she prepared breakfast for everyone in the kitchen.

"Do you need some help, Nala?"

Nala looked surprised.

"Oh my! young man, you're up so early this morning, aren't you tired from all that excitement yesterday?"

"Well, I am a little, but I'm too excited to stay in bed," he smiled.

"Well, we can go collect some eggs from the hen house if you like, right after you've showered," Nala laughed directing him to the bathroom.

Kam showered in super quick time, returned to the kitchen, and drank the fresh milk Nala had set out for him. "Right, where's this hen house then?"

"Follow me," Nala summoned.

Nala led Kam outside, and down to the bottom of the garden.

"Wow, you can see the football pitch from here Nala!"

Nala smiled, "Dave's right, you really are obsessed with this football lark aren't you, Kam?"

"It's not a lark Nala, football is just the best thing in the whole world!" he exclaimed, "If it wasn't for football, I wouldn't have so many friends, and I wouldn't be here in Migos meeting even more friends, would I?"

"You know what Kam?", you're right, "I've never thought about it like that before."

Kam continued "All over the world people come together to play and follow football and it may be the only thing they have in common but that doesn't matter, it brings them all together."

"One World! One World!,"

"Morning Ethan, what's that you're singing?" asked Nala.

"Have you heard of Will. I. Am and the Black-Eyed Peas?" he asked.

"I heard what you just said about football, I'm just saying what Will.I.Am always says, "We've only got one world!"

Kam laughed, "He's a big Will. I. Am fan and 'Where Is the love' is his favourite song, but suppose it fits with what we are trying to do with our new football team.

"I see, laughed Nala, "but let's get these eggs before everyone comes down for breakfast".

Ethan's eyes lit up, "Mm breakfast!"

"Oh, and Ethan is always hungry too," Kam informed Nala, "I think he loves food almost as much as I love football." he laughed.

Nala made scrambled eggs, with sausage and baked beans, while Kam and Ethan prepared some homemade bread, by the time everyone arrived for breakfast the table had been laid beautifully by the two boys.

"Wow," said Katie, "this looks amazing, I'll expect more of this when we get home," she laughed.

Dave pulled out a chair for her to sit next to him and everyone sat down to eat.

After breakfast, Diego and Ano offered to clear the table, not realising there would be no dishwasher in the kitchen. "What did we do?" laughed Ano to Diego when they realised. "This is going to take ages!"

"You, and your bright ideas!" Diego puffed as he stacked the plates next to the sink.

"Turn that frown upside down 'D'" laughed Ano as he blew a handful of bubbles towards him. "Come on it won't take long then we'll have the rest of the day to see what kind of music they play around here."

"Yeah, good idea Ano, let's see what they think of the music we produce too?

Mid-morning, Bako took his visitors on a tour of the village introducing them to everyone they met. Typically, Kam took a ball along, kicking it around and showing off his ball skills as he went, much to the delight of some of the younger children as they joined in with him. They were welcomed everywhere they went, but strangely, when Bako introduced Dave to some of the villagers, he kept getting the same comment, that he looked familiar but couldn't quite remember where they'd seen him before. Dave thought maybe they'd seen him on T.V. playing football when he was younger, I mean I haven't aged much in the last twenty years, he laughed to himself.

When they arrived back at Bako's house a few hours later, Nala was sitting on the front porch relaxing.

"Did you all have a good time?" she asked.

"Yes, thank you, Nala," the boys replied in unison.

"Would you like a cold drink? You must be thirsty," she asked.

"Yes, please Auntie," said Ano, "But we'll get the drinks, you look so relaxed there, we'll come back and relax with you." And that's what they did, everyone gathered on the porch for the afternoon, drinking, snacking, talking, laughing, and a good time was had by all.

Kam had been asking the time all afternoon, making sure he wouldn't be late for training. At 5.30pm Kam ran upstairs to get changed, closely followed by Ethan, ten minutes later they ran back downstairs, Astro trainers in hand.

"We're ready Dave, are you coming?".

Dave looked at Kam and smiled.

"I will be in 10 mins or so, you carry on and I'll meet you on the pitch, it looks like your new friends are waiting for you." Sure enough, sitting on the porch steps were Darnell-Lessi, Marc-Bashford, Caetano-Donaldo, Samuel-Bronson, Pele-Ali and Arnold-Alexander.

"Hey guys, we're so looking forward to this!" grinned

Kam. The boys chatted as they made their way to the training pitch, and as they turned the corner the goal nets were just going up. The boys made their way over to the goal area, eager to introduce Kam and Ethan to their coach, the man putting up the nets. As the man turned around Kam and Ethan were so surprised...."Whoa! Dave, thought you weren't ready yet? And what have you done? Where has your famous afro disappeared to? and where did that beard come from?" laughed Kam.

"Dave? Who is Dave?" said the man in a Nigerian accent.

"Why are you talking like that? You're such a joker Dave! but it's not the best disguise" Kam and Ethan were laughing so hard they had to sit down before they fell down. But, as they looked up, they saw a familiar figure walking across the pitch towards them, it was Dave.

"Wait a minute if that's Dave then who is that?" asked Ethan.

"I don't know but I think we're about to find out," replied Kam.

As Dave came closer, he stopped dead in his tracks, the two men stood still staring at each other, both speechless. Kam noticed Dave's eyes begin to fill up with tears.

"You ok boss? You look like you have seen a ghost".

The two men walked closer, embracing, wrapping their

arms around each other, both now in floods of tears, happy tears. "My brother! My brother!" the man blurted out. They each took a step back to look at their long-lost brother.

"Ade, I always dreamed this day would come, I can't believe you're here." Dave sobbed wiping away the tears trickling down his face.

"Will someone tell us what's going on?" frowned Kam. "This is my dad and our football coach, Ade," said Darnell-Lessi, "He told us a long time ago that he had a twin brother, but we didn't believe him, he didn't know how he knew he was just always so sure about it, he always said the other half of him was missing, he wasn't sure what had happened to him but he always said he would come home one day, it looks like today's the day".

"Wow! exclaimed Kam, "Dave told us he had a twin brother too, this is unbelievable, and fantastic!"

Dave and Ade were now laughing uncontrollably, still wiping away those happy tears, both in disbelief that they had finally found each other after all these years. Dave explained to Ade how and why he and his friends had come to be in Migos.

Ade explained "my father had found me as a small boy wandering by myself near to his house all those years ago kicking a football down the road. Dad asked around his village, but no one knew why I was there or where I came from. The only words I could say were 'football' and my name 'Ade'. My father and his wife had wanted a child of their own for so long, but it had never happened to them. Then when I suddenly appeared from no-where, well, they thought I was a gift from God, so they took me in and brought me up as their own. I had a great childhood, my father was a football coach too, he travelled all over coaching the best teams in Africa, even reaching the semi-finals of the Africa Cup of Nations on two occasions. When he retired from football, he and my mother decided to settle in Migos. I moved away to train as a teacher and I began coaching football too, I came back when my mother became ill, my parents live just over there, they would be so happy to meet you. Not long after I came back, I met a beautiful girl called 'Esme', we fell in love and got married and we decided to make our home in the village. I began teaching at the village school and then started up my own football training camp and the rest, as they say, is history. It's as if all of this was meant to be. All I can think of now is how glad I am to finally see my brother after all these years."

"Now I realise why I felt so at home here because I am home." smiled Dave. "Why don't you bring Esme and your mum and dad round to Bako's house for supper later? I'll introduce you to Katie."

"Is Katie your wife Dave?" asked Ade. "No, she's my next-door neighbour and mum to Diego, Kam and Ethan," smiled Dave, "but she is the woman I want to spend the rest of my life with, she's wonderful, but I just haven't had the courage to tell her yet."

"Well, no time like the present, what are you waiting

for?" laughed Ade, "just go for it, she sounds like 'the one' to me."

"Hey you guys, we're waiting!" Dave and Ade turned around to find the boys had lined up waiting for their training session to begin.

"Wow, you're eager aren't you" laughed Ade, "but before we start, I want to introduce to someone else too," Ade summoned a small boy over who'd been sitting on the touchline watching the boys warm up.

"This is my other son Evan-Havard."

"Well hello Evan-Havard, good to meet you," smiled Dave shaking Evan-Havard's hand.

"Good to meet you too sir," replied Evan-Havard.

"Are you going to join us for training today too?" asked Dave.

"No sir, I don't play football, you see my feet aren't very good, I have Cerebral Palsy which means I can't run around for very long."

Dave looked down at the young boy.

"I see," Dave looked at Ade, "Well Evan-Havard, just because you aren't up to playing football it doesn't mean you can't get involved, there's a whole lot more to a football team than just the players. There are some very, very important jobs to be done off the pitch also, I think you should become our kit man, after this training session we need to get together for an executive meeting and discuss our new kit design, I'm sure you'll have lots of great ideas."

Evan-Havard lifted his hand towards Dave, high-fived him and smiled. "I'll get right on it Dave, I'll see you later then." Evan-Havard took a note pad and pencil from his bag, sat down behind the goals, and began to sketch and make his notes grinning from ear to ear.

"This is going to be one hell of a training session!" exclaimed Pele-Ali," if your coach is as good as our coach then we're going to have the best team in the world!" he shouted, punching the air.

Ade and Dave looked at each other.

"Shall we do this Ade?"

"I can't think of anything I'd rather do, Dave! Let's go!"

By this time lots of children had turned up to watch the training session. Dave and Ade turned to face the boys, Ade wiped a tear from his eye and cleared his throat.

"Right, you lot, we've got a job to do, we are going to the "YOUTH WORLD CUP!" The boys went crazy, jumping up and down, crazy dance moves, goal celebrations, the boys were hardly able to control themselves.

"Ok! Ok!" Laughed Kam, "Come on! the hard work starts now!"

The boys lined up, grinning from ear to ear, and so the training for the best football competition in the world began.

Once the boys had finished their pre-training stretches

and ran a couple of circuits around the pitch, Dave and Ade laid out cones, slalom poles, hurdles, and ladders, encouraging their balance, speed, reacting under pressure, first touch and control, and awareness of players around them. They practiced shooting with a target sheet hung between the goalposts. Dave commented "I wouldn't want to be in goal in front of these boys!" when he saw how hard and accurately some of the boys were hitting the ball. The long-lost brothers nodded to each other, each knowing exactly what the other was thinking, that this was an exciting, determined, skillful bunch of boys, with the real potential of reaching and should they dare to dream of winning the World Cup".

After training the boys burst into Bako's house, closely followed by Dave.

"Whoa!!" what's going on?" shouted Bako, "what's the rush?".

"Have we got news for you," said Dave, he turned to the boys, "You guys go and shower before supper and I'll explain to Bako, Nala and your mum the brilliant news and what a wonderful day we've had."

The boys ran upstairs.

"I'm first in the shower!" exclaimed Ethan, "Just in case supper is early?"

Kam shook his head, "Do you ever think about anything but food Ethan?" he laughed.

"Yes, I do," replied Ethan sounding serious. "I've been

thinking about hearing Dave tell Ade that he wants to marry mum but he's too scared to ask her, it really would be great, but I think he needs our help,"

"Wow! I'm sure we can think of something," winked Kam, "Let's go tell Diego, he's the brains of the family, he'll know what to do."

Ade and Esme, Darnell-Lessi, and Evan-Havard came round for supper, along with Ade's Mum and Dad who were so happy to see the long-lost brothers getting to know each other, they told Dave lots of stories about Ade growing up and how he always had a ball at his feet, football was a big part of his childhood and now it seems it had an even bigger part to play.

Bako and Nala's house was filled with so much laughter that evening and brimming with love between the newfound family and friends. Katie couldn't help but look around and see her boys so happy, she turned to look at Dave and realised just how much this man had come to mean to her and the boys, she felt happy and content and realised she had come to love this kind, humble, big-hearted man, how on Earth was she going to let him know how she felt?

CHAPTER 11

TEAM SELECTION

The boys trained daily for two whole weeks, and the more they got to know and like each other the better they played, it was if they'd always been a team, there was a real sense of excitement around the village. Towards the end of the second weeks training, it seemed like every man, woman, and child from the village were at the training sessions, shouting and chanting words of encouragement, singing, and dancing, there was a real buzz around the place, the boys felt like superstars.

After the final training session, Dave told the boys to go home but asked them to meet him on the porch of Bako and Nala's house at 6 pm that evening, where he would decide which players, he would be taking to the World Cup Tournament. The boys were so eager to find out who Dave and Ade had chosen to join the team, they arrived at 5 pm, along with the boys' parents and what seemed to be the whole village, who'd come to wish them all good luck, the suspense was too much, they sat in silence on the porch waiting for Dave and Ade's big announcement. They didn't have to wait long, Kam and Ethan joined the rest of the boys on the porch, Diego and Ano sat down alongside Katie, Bako, and Nala on the porch bench and Dave and Ade appeared. "Well, boys! We will not keep you in suspense any longer. We've drawn up the team sheet and this is what we've decided".

Dave called out the names of the players they had chosen.

1. Zach Brealish (goalkeeper) Academy player

2. Samuel-Bronson (left-back)

3. Arnold-Alexander (centre-back)

4. Barry Payne (right-back) Academy Player

5. Pele-Ali (centre-mid)

6. Marc-Bashford (right mid)

7. Kam St. Clair (left-wing) Academy player

8. Jacob-Rivermore (centre-mid) Academy player

9. Raheem Mervyn (Striker) Academy player

10. Darnell-Lessi (Striker)

11. Caetano-Donaldo (right-wing)

12. Ethan St. Clair (centre-mid) Academy player

The boys looked at each other, huge grins appeared on their faces.

"That's right boys, you're ALL going to the World Cup!", bellowed Dave.

"YAAAAY!" The boys leapt to their feet, punching the air, screaming, and shouting with delight, hugging, and congratulating each other, the whole village erupted with excitement, drums were beating, everyone singing and dancing, small children running around laughing.

Dave continued "Boys, we will need a few more players

to make up the whole squad but we have a plan for that," he turned to Kam and winked, Kam winked back, he knew exactly what Dave meant.

Katie got up and gave Dave a humongous hug,

"What's that for?" he smiled, blushing slightly.

Katie looked up at Dave "For making my boys so happy, I've never seen them so excited, and if they're happy I'm happy." "They make me happy too you know, smiled Dave, they've become like family to me, and being here makes me realise just how important family and good friends are, it's the good people in your life that count, the people you love and the people that love you, they are your real family and that's all that matters."

Dave took Katie's hand, "Come on, let's get a drink from the kitchen, thirsty work this is,"

"What is?" asked Katie,

"Getting all soppy," laughed Dave.

"Ethan is right," Katie smiled to herself, "there really is only 'One big Dave'."

As they entered the kitchen Diego called out from the dining room, "Mum! Dave! could you come here for a minute please, I need your help?"

Mum and Dave walked over to the dining room to find Diego, Ano, Kam, and Ethan standing arms folded in front of the dining table.

"What's up boys?" Dave asked.

"Absolutely nothing," grinned Kam.

Ano bowed "We've got a surprise for you,".

"TADA!" laughed Ethan.

The boys had set up the table for a romantic meal, lit candles, and all.

"We'll be your waiters for the evening," said Diego, "I'm sure Nala will have some leftovers from dinner, we'll be right back."

Dave and Katie sat down, looked at each other and laughed, "Well this is kind of romantic don't you think," said Dave blushing again.

"There's nothing wrong with a little romance," replied Katie.

The boys came back, walking one behind the other, tea towels across their arms, Diego with the chicken, Kam with the rice, Ano with the salad and Ethan with the wine.

"If there's anything else you need for this very 'SPECIAL' evening, please let us know we'll be right outside." Grinned Kam

"I'm sure we'll be fine," spluttered Dave, it had suddenly dawned on him that the boys had overheard his conversation with his brother earlier at training.

"You ok Dave?" asked Katie, "You seem a little flustered,"

"I'm fine," he smiled, "I'm here with you, I've never

been happier."

"I'm happy too," smiled Katie.

"Well, I'm glad about that," said Dave shyly, "Because there's something I've been wanting to ask you for quite some time now,"

"Don't tell me, you want me to start washing those smelly football kits again, is your washing machine on the blink again, I mean I don't mind really, but"..........

Dave put his finger to his lips, "Shh! If I don't do this now, I don't know when I'll pluck up the courage again," Dave got down on one knee, took a small box from his pocket and cleared his throat, "Katie, I love you, and have done for a very long time now, you're an amazing mum, and an amazing friend and I'm wondering if you'd like to be my amazing wife?"

Dave opened the small box and took out a handmade, brightly coloured ring, "it's not the most expensive ring Katie, but I saw you admiring it yesterday in that little jewelry shop at the bottom of the hill, it's just a small token until we get back to England, Katie, will you marry me?"

"Katie looked at Dave with tears in her eyes, "Yes, I would love to!"

Dave slipped the ring on Katies' finger.

"It's perfect!" smiled Katie.

The door burst open, and the boys fell over themselves onto the dining room floor.

"Well, you've heard the good news then boys," laughed Dave. "Then say hello to my future wife!"

"Group hug then," smiled Katie, "I'm so happy I could burst!"

When they'd all calmed down, they made their way out onto the porch to join the others and gave them the good news. Bako fetched champagne from the fridge and the celebrations went on into the early hours until one by one the villagers returned to their homes, and the boys retired to bed exhausted, especially at the thought of the all the hard work they were going to have to put in to prepare for the World Cup Tournament.

CHAPTER 12

MAKING PLANS

The next morning everyone sat down for breakfast, Ade, Darnell-Lessi and Evan-Havard had joined them.

Darnell -Lessi sat next to Kam and the excitement for the tournament began to build. It was decided that they would travel to England by the end of the week and all the boys' parents needed to be informed of their plans.

It was four weeks from the Youth World Cup group stages and Well Borne All Stars were to play their first match on Monday 1st July. The list of things to do seemed endless, there were the kits to sort, new boots for the players and travel arrangements to be made.

Dave and Ade sat on the porch discussing their plans. The job in hand was exciting but daunting all the same.

"How are we going to pay for all this? Football kits are expensive and football boots don't come cheap." frowned Dave.

"Better get our thinking caps on, we've not got much time. I'll make a few calls to the lads at the academy and let them know what we need and see if they can find a few sponsors to help us out."

"No need for that!"

Dave and Ade turned round to find a group of teenagers had gathered behind them.

"Hello, my name is Jol, and these are my friends, Kizzy, Zina and Jaali. We attend the local college, studying art and design. We'd like to make your team kit if you'll allow us. It won't cost you anything, we've discussed it with the principal already and he's agreed the college will supply the materials. It would be a great project for us and a way of showing the world our designs, we've got some great ideas and we've got a new little student who has been helping us with some amazing ideas, his name is Evan-Havard" Dave and Ade looked at each other, then looked over at Evan-Havard and smiled.

"Sounds like a win-win situation to me." Replied Dave and Ade simultaneously, "Wow! We really are twins, aren't we?" they laughed.

"Well, I think you've got yourself a deal." said Ade.

"We'll come round this evening, and we'll bring you the samples of the kits we've already made a start on and by the end of the week we'll have them all finished no problem," smiled Jol.

"Fantastic, we'll look forward to seeing them, that just leaves the boots to sort." smiled Dave.

"Well actually," interrupted Jol, "My brother Chuk has a workshop on the other side of the village, he designs and makes shoes, he sells them in the city, he's a very successful designer."

"Are you kidding me?" Dave gasped, "You really are a talented bunch aren't you," he smiled.

"He asked me to show you these football boots, he's been working on them since the day you arrived." Jol passed Dave the box containing the boots and as he opened the box, he could not believe his eyes.

"Wow! Wow! These are amazing, superb! I've never seen boots quite like these before, wait until the boys see them." The bright, white boots had been embroidered with every team flag that was taking part in the World Cup Tournament. Even the laces were rainbow coloured.

"It's almost a shame to wear them, they really are a work of art! I think we need to meet your brother, could you ask him to meet us here at 5 pm this evening too? grinned Dave.

"Sure," replied Jol, "I'll call him now, we'll see you all later, 5pm sharp."

Dave and Ade returned to the dining room, "Oh shucks! we were going to offer to clear the table and wash up, but it looks like you boys have beat us to it," Dave laughed.

"Yeah, a likely story," frowned Ethan.

"Well, we're looking at new kits for the tournament later so if you boys are planning on doing anything today could you be back for 5 pm please?" asked Ade.

"We'll be out the back having a kick around," said Darnell.

"I should have guessed," laughed Dave, "Ok! See you later."

Dave and Katie made the most of the non-training day, they spent the day together, their first real date, holding hands, wandering around the village before sitting down for something to eat and a cold beer at one of the local food shacks. Before they knew it, it was time to head back to finalise the plans for the tournament.

"When we get back to England, I'll take you out somewhere special to celebrate our engagement," said Dave taking hold of Katie's hand.

"This is all the celebration I need," replied Katie, "What could be more special than this place, being surrounded by the most important people in my life, you, the boys, family, that's what matters, I've never felt happier than I do right now ....and when we win the World Cup, that will be the icing on the cake," she laughed. "Wembley Stadium here we come!"

After dinner that evening Dave, Ade, Jol, and his friends and Chuk revealed the new kit and boots to the boys, the kit matched the boots perfectly, the tops consisted of a white background with every team flag embroidered around all the edges of the tops, plain white shorts flags edged around the bottom of the shorts, and white socks and the matching tracksuits were superb. The boys were brimming with excitement as it was but when they saw their new kit for once they were speechless.

"I don't know what to say," said Kam.

"Well, there's a first time for everything," laughed Dave.

Kam stood up, "On behalf of my teammates and I, thank you so much! they're amazing!" He turned to the rest of the boys "We're going to shine boys, in more ways than one," he shouted. The boys took turns shaking hands and thanking the designers.

"This deserves a toast," said Dave, "Everyone raise your glasses, to each and every one who is helping make this dream come true, I thank you from the bottom of my heart."

"And, to the best kit man we've ever had Evan-Havard!" shouted Kam "THANK YOU!"

CHAPTER 13

ON OUR WAY

Friday soon arrived; it was time to go back to England for the big event. Everything was packed and stacked up on the front porch ready to go.

The boys and their families had arrived, everyone was set to go. The whole village had turned out to see them off, Dave felt sad that he would not be able to take all this support with them but unbeknown to him Ade had a real surprise for him.

Dave took out the magic ball from the kit bag and everyone gathered round ready to link arms.

"Wait, wait!" shouted Ade, Ade reached inside his backpack and pulled out ....an IDENTICAL BALL!......

Dave gasped "Oh wow! Where did you get that?

"Well, began Ade, "My father gave it to me when I moved back here, he said it was the ball I was playing with when he found me all those years ago, when you told me about the ball you found in your garage, I realised It was exactly the same as the one in my house. That evening I went home and tested the ball to see if it was just as magical as yours, but it didn't work...until Darnell-Lessi decided to give it a go and guess what? MAGIC!!, It probably explains why my father couldn't find my real parents because that ball had transported me so far away from home, if the only word I could say was 'football' it transported me to the nearest football coach, that being my father. It seems the magic has been passed on to the next generation. And it got me thinking, if we have the magic twice what's stopping us from taking all this support with us?" asked Ade.

"I can't think of a single thing brother" replied Dave.

Dave and Ade turned around and shouted, "Everyone, link arms, we're all going to ENGLAND!"

Once everyone had stopped jumping up and down with excitement they linked arms, and simultaneously Kam and Darnell-Lessi threw the two magic balls into the air, as the balls fell to the boys' feet they shouted, " Well Borne St, Well Borne, England!" …….. WHOOSH! WHOOSH! ……. after what seemed like seconds Dave, Katie, Ade, Esme, Mr. Abara, Bako, Nala, the boys, and the entire village arrived outside Dave and Katie's houses, everyone cheered and hugged each other, suddenly doors began to open, people began wandering out of their homes, suddenly Dave looked worried.

"Katie, I think we should have thought this through a little better, where are all these people going to stay?"

"I've got a spare room," called out grumpy Mr. Smith.

Maybe he's not so grumpy after all, thought Kam, he's not grumpy, he's just lonely he thought to himself, maybe next time my ball lands in his garden I'll go and say hello instead of shouting from behind the fence.

"Me too! I've got a spare room," shouted Mr. Chopra from number 67. Amazingly, one by one the neighbours offered to help, it brought tears to Dave's eyes, "you really are amazing, thank you."

"You just bring that cup home," laughed Mr. Chopra, "And we've been expecting you."

Mr. Abara looked over at his wife Kesanda and Ano's

97

sister Sade.

"You can't keep a secret can you?" Ano laughed, "Thanks Mum!"

Dave and Ade made sure everyone had somewhere to stay, then Dave showed Ade and his mum and dad, Esme, Darnell-Lessi, and Evan-Havard into his home. They entered the living room and as soon as Ade saw the elderly couple sitting on the sofa he burst into tears, he knew exactly who they were, ... "Mom!... Dad!" Dave gave his mum and dad a hug, wiping away his tears, "I'll leave you to get to know your son and his family again Mum, and I'll see you all in the morning."

Dave headed next door and helped Katie unpack before they slumped down onto the sofa exhausted.

"You do realise we need a few more players to complete the squad, don't you?" Dave asked sheepishly.

Mum knew what Dave was trying to say, "Don't worry I know what you need to do, you go, just take good care of my boy, I'll stay and sort the rest of the arrangements."

The next morning, Dave and Kam were all prepared for their next journey to find five more players to make up the rest of the squad.

"We'll be back in a few days mum, and don't worry about us, we'll be fine," he smiled excitedly.

"I'll be fine too," she replied, "I've got enough to keep me busy until you get back, now gives us a hug you two, and hurry back."

They went out into the back garden, out came the magic ball and, WHOOSH! WHOOSH! Kam and Dave were gone.

CHAPTER 14

THE BUILD UP

While they were away Katie, Esme and Ade made all the arrangements for the upcoming matches, they booked the team coach, Evan-Havard checked the kits were all packed, tracksuits were ready, and the boots were in the correct players' bag, they arranged the training sessions, and the first aid kit was checked.

Ade trained the boys harder than they'd ever trained before, the boy's parents and the Migos villagers came every day to encourage them, Mr. Smith came and helped make flags and banners to wave pitch side with his newfound friends, not that the boys needed any more encouragement, they were enjoying every moment of training, they knew what the end goal was, to be 'World Champions!'

During the third day of training, the doors of the gym flung open,

"Hey guys!", "Remember us?" They had returned, Dave and Kam stood grinning from ear to ear, behind them a group of boys they had not seen before.

"Well, we did it! We've completed the squad!" shouted Kam, "Let me introduce you to:

'Edgar Dravid' from Holland, 'Lemar Jnr' from Brazil, 'Joe Salla' from Egypt, 'Aiden Bayor' from Iran and 'Tevin Dejoyner' from Germany."

Katie gave Kam an enormous hug and a kiss on the cheek, much to Kam's embarrassment in front of the boys, then turned to Dave, he got the same treatment, but there was no complaint from him.

The boys introduced themselves and before Dave could say "Do you want a kick about?' The boys' jackets were off, Astro trainers were on and off they went. The big man was impressed.

"I like their enthusiasm, this has got to be the best team I've ever worked with, the skills, the fitness, the positivity, they're amazing, I can't wait for the tournament!"

The boys trained daily for the next two weeks, alternating between fitness training including beep tests, sprinting, burpees, squats, skipping and anything they could think of to keep the boys at their best. Football training consisted of cone exercises, shooting from a square pass, one-touch shooting, lay-offs, turns, chest control, running with the ball, throw-ins, heading the ball, tackling, the list was endless and repetitive but necessary, and as everyone knows, practice makes perfect.

At the end of the second week, the boys were exhausted but happy, feeling confident, they had really gelled as a team, each boy brought a different kind of strength and skill to the team, each one complimenting the other.

Dave and Ade called the boys to them for the final team talk before the tournament,

"Well boys, that's all we can do now before the tournament begins, you are the best team I've ever had the pleasure of working with and to think you hardly knew each other a few weeks ago. It just goes to prove that no matter who you are or where you're from, no matter what language you speak, if you're rich or poor, if you have one thing in common, we can become one! Thank you all for your hard work and commitment. No matter what happens, win, or lose, I'm proud of each and every one of you"

The boys were silent for all but a few seconds.... Then the chanting started "Big Dave! there's only one Big Dave!!, there's only one big Dave!" Dave was moved to tears, he could not remember being this proud, ever!

ALMOST THERE

The boys sailed through the group stages no problem and found themselves through to the quarter finals, they were super excited, just three matches away from the Youth World Cup Final.

The draw for the remaining eight teams were drawn:

Manchester Dynamos -V- Well Borne All Stars

Juventus Tigers -V- Liverpool Avengers

Sporting Madrid -V- Chelski Utd

Barca Demons -V- Paris Youth FC

The boys finished training on Thursday evening, buzzing at the thought of playing at Old Trafford in the next round. "Right, you lot, go home and rest, eat properly, no late nights and no computer games they're too much of a distraction, I want you fully focused on the next game, be sure to be at the academy for 10.00 am on Saturday, the coach will be taking us to Old Trafford for the first game against Manchester Dynamos, Kick-off 3 pm!" The boys high-fived each other,

"All-Stars by name! All-Stars by nature!" shouted Darnell-Lessi, "We can do this! One team! One dream!" shouted Ethan.

Kam grinned "Hey, I like it, wished I'd thought of that," he laughed, "Right boys, that's the team motto from now on". The boys joined hands and raised them in the air,

"AII-STARS BY NAME, ALL-STARS BY NATURE, ONE TEAM, ONE DREAM!"

Kam and Ethan spent all day Friday, as usual, practicing their skills in the garden, music blaring from the back bedroom where Diego and Ano were creating their music and Mum and Esme made lunch while Dave and Ade prepared for tomorrow's game.

As soon as they all sat down for lunch Dave's phone rang, by the look on Dave's face Kam knew something was very wrong, "Ok, thanks for letting me know, hope he's ok and I'll pop round after the game tomorrow to see how he is," Dave hung up, sat down, and held his head in his hands.

Now Kam was worried. "What's happened, boss?"

"That was Zach Brealish's mum, it looks like Zach's sprained his wrist, he tripped over his little sisters' toys earlier and fell heavily on to his arm he's currently in A & E but it's not looking good."

Kam's eye began to fill up with tears, "but he's our only goalkeeper! That's it, we're done for!"

Kam ran upstairs and threw himself onto his bed, the tears streaming down his face.

Dave followed him upstairs and sat on the bed beside him. "Kam, we've not come this far to give up now, we'll find a way."

"How? without a goalkeeper, we'll lose every game!" Now the tears were really flowing.

Dave handed Kam a tissue, "Dry your eyes Kam, we're going to sort this, I promise."

"Don't tell anyone I was crying Dave; they'll think I'm a baby."

Dave gave Kam a hug, "Hey big man, you think men don't cry too, we're only human you know," he laughed, trying to lift Kam's mood.

Kam wiped away the tears, "Well, I haven't cried like this since my dad left."

"Well, that must have been a sad time so of course you would have been upset,"

"No Dave you don't understand,"

"What do you mean Kam, talk to me."

"A few years ago, my dad was being really unkind to Mum, and she used to cry, a lot, in the end he left, we had to sell our house and that's when we moved here.

I do get to see my dad now and everything is cool with him and Mum but for a long time I did miss having Dad around to play football with me. When I joined the academy, it made me really happy, that's why I got so angry and upset, I feel like everything is going to go wrong again, and I'm sorry and all that but this competition is everything to me."

Dave looked down at Kam, he hated seeing this usually happy and smiley boy looking so sad, "I'm sorry to hear that Kam, I didn't realise, but you can talk to me at any time you know that right? day or night. I can't replace your dad, but I'll be there for you whenever you need me, I promise. Now I'm going to let Ade know what's happened, and let's see what we can come up with."

"Thanks Dave, I believe in you, I'll be down in a minute."

Kam had just returned to the table when Mum blurted out, "I know a goalkeeper without a club, I met them at the hospital last week, they're 12 years old, and used to play for Chelski Utd up until a couple of years ago, would you like me to give their mum a call?" Dave almost spats out his drink, he'd been pacing up and down trying to figure out where they'd find a goalkeeper at such short notice. "Well, of course, call them now, there's no time to waste!"

Mum left the room and within five minutes she was back, looking serious. Kam, fingers crossed under the table, waiting with bated breath for what she was going to say. "They'll be here within the hour!"

Kam breathed a sigh of relief and his eyes filled up once again, Dave winking "Told you, we'll be fine, now let's clear the table, make ourselves busy, that hour will pass in the blink of an eye.

Everyone had gathered on the patio when there was a knock at the door; Mum quickly got up, "I'll get it." Kam, Ethan, Dave, and Ade sat nervously until she returned.

"Let me introduce you to Brogan, Brogan Pitford and her mum Julia." Dave stood up and shook their hands.

"Pleased to meet you both, hopefully, you're the answer to our prayers." Kam looked up, before him stood a girl, in full goalkeeper gear, gloves and cap included, and on her feet, two blades that Kam thought looked like boomerangs. Dave called to Kam, "Kam, come and say hello."

Kam stood up, almost in tears again. "How can she be in our team?"

Brogan glared at him, "What do you mean? Why do you say that? Because I wear these blades?"

"No, because you're a girl, I've never seen a girl play for any of Joseph Romenio's teams," Kam replied crossly.

Brogan glared at Kam, "Well, that's because I played for Chelski Utd girls' team, and before I became ill, we hadn't lost a match all season, so be quiet and dry your eyes!"

Kam wasn't impressed at all. "Well maybe that's because you were playing against girls' teams."

"Kam St. Clair! Don't be so rude!"

Kam knew he was in big trouble when mum called him by his full name.

"So, what happened to your feet then?" Kam asked sheepishly.

"Glad you asked Kam, at least you didn't just stand and stare, that just makes me mad," then she explained.

"Two years ago, I fell from my bicycle and cut my leg, then it got infected, it was really, really, painful but I didn't realise how unwell it was making me until I woke up in hospital a week later, that's when mum told me

110

the infection had gotten really bad, I became so poorly that they had to amputate my feet to save my life. I didn't think I'd ever play football again and Chelski Utd terminated my contract. I think I cried non-stop for two whole days. But gradually I became stronger and stronger, then I got my blades fitted, I felt stronger than ever and thought I can either just sit around and feel sorry for myself or I can show them I'm just as good as I was before if not better because I'm more determined than ever to be the best, I don't have a number one on my back to be second best you know! I've been back in training with the help of Jordan Banks for six months now."

Kam felt embarrassed, "Wow! Jordan Banks? He's a legend, the best keeper England ever had, I'm so sorry about what I said before, really I am, he said sheepishly, I've just never watched girls play football before, and this tournament means the world to me."

Brogan smiled "You're ok, boys can be mean sometimes, but if you give me a chance, I'll show you just what THIS girl can do!"

Kam couldn't help thinking Brogan was a little bossy but also how pretty she was when she smiled, her long brown hair divided into two long plaits, and her sparkling blue eyes....'pull yourself together he thought to himself, she's just a girl.'

Dave nudged Mum, "I think Kam likes our new keeper,"

"I think he does too" mum smiled.

Dave picked up his car keys "No time like the present

guys, come on, let's get down to the academy and introduce Brogan to the rest of the team."

Kam looked excited "Excellent idea Boss, come on Ethan grab your boots this is going to be interesting, and don't worry Brogan the other boys won't give you any hassle, I'll make sure of that."

Brogan smiled, "Don't worry about me Kam, I'm tougher than I look, and they're going to be so impressed they'll wonder how they ever managed without me."

The training session went better than anyone could have ever expected, Brogan was outstanding, it was obvious she hadn't let her injury get in the way of her dreams, not many of the boys put a ball past her, they couldn't have been more impressed though they felt sad for Zach, he'd returned from hospital following his x-ray, it was clear his arm was badly sprained and he'd be out for the rest of the tournament, he sat on the bench with his arm in a sling, he was sad he wasn't going to play and felt bad for letting the team down, but watching Brogan's diving and stretching, her fingertip saves and her command of the six-yard box, even he had to admit Brogan Pitford was the perfect replacement.

Everyone went home happy and excited about tomorrow's game. Kam would sleep well tonight, safe in the knowledge the team was complete yet again.

CHAPTER 16

THE QUARTER FINALS

The All-Stars dressed in their new, bright, colourful tracksuits arrived at Old Trafford to a wall of flags and banners being waived by their friends, families, and neighbours, the noise was deafening, so many smiling faces, it was an unbelievable sight, they were escorted to their dressing room, passing all the trophy cabinets, but the boys weren't intimidated by this amazing stadium, it just made them even more determined to beat one of the best youth teams in the world.

"We'll show them" shouted Kam, "We might not be the most expensive team in the competition, we may not have a stadium like this to play in every week but what we have got is skills, strength and determination like no other team but most of all we've got each other, we're friends first and foremost, remember "All-Stars by name, All-Stars by nature! One team, One dream!"

In the dressing room, Evan-Havard, dressed in his new tracksuit with his initials on the front and Assistant Manager on the back, he felt he'd worked so hard he deserved a promotion so had promoted himself to Assistant Manager and no-one could disagree with that, he'd placed the new kits on hooks above the benches and their boots gleaming below, the boys changed quickly then Dave and Ade stood up and announced the first eleven players and the subs:

1. Brogan Pitford (goalkeeper)

2. Samuel-Bronson (left-back)

3. Arnold-Alexander (centre-back)

4. Barry Payne (right-back)

5. Pele-Ali (centre-mid)

6. Marc-Bashford (right mid)

7. Kam St. Clair (left-wing)

8. Jacob-Rivermore (centre-mid)

9. Raheem Mervyn (striker)

10. Darnell-Lessi (striker)

11. Caetano-Donaldo (right-wing)

Subs: 12. Joe Salah, 14. Edgar Dravid, 15. Lemar Jnr, 16. Aiden Bayor, 17. Ethan St. Clair 18. Tevin Dejoyner

Ade continued, "Right lads, I know no one wants to be substitute but you've all got a big part to play over these last three games, I'm confident we're going all the way in this tournament, so come on Well Borne, let's show the world what being a team is all about!"

Five minutes before kick-off the dressing room door opened, and they were summoned out into the tunnel. Lining up alongside Manchester Dynamos the boys stood heads held high, focused on the job in hand, walking out onto the pitch to the roar of a packed stadium, and the people making the most noise, not surprisingly, were the Well Borne All Stars fans, the flags and the banners were spectacularly colourful, they really were doing the team proud.

The commentators for the game Ian Wright, Rio Chopramand, and the two Gary's, Neville and Lineker, commented on the spectacular display put on by the Well Bourne All Stars fans. "I can't help but think with this kind of support from their fans, it could just give Well Bourne or should I call them the 'ALL STARS' a bit of an edge over the Dynamos this afternoon," grinned Ian.

"No chance!" replied Neville, "They've not played together long enough, this Manchester team have been training for this for months, been playing together for years."

"I've got to agree with you Ian," Rio butted in, "As much as I'd like to see Manchester lift this cup, I've seen what these boys are capable of and believe me I think we could be in for a bit of a surprise this afternoon. I can see why they're called 'ALL STARS'."

The teams lined up, shook hands, and prepared for kick-off. Dynamos were to kick off first.

The referee took his whistle from his pocket and blew!

Dynamos began passing the ball between themselves for a couple of minutes, teasing the All-Stars to come and get it, showing off, but the All-Stars were patient and started closing the opposition down, pressing further and further up the pitch until all of a sudden, the Dynamos left back made a bad back pass to their goalkeeper, the goalkeeper miss-kicked and it went out for an All Stars corner. The crowd roared, COME ON ALL STARS!!, COME ON ALL STARS!!

Kam ran over to take the left-hand corner, leaving Pele-Ali and Jacob-Rivermore just in front of the halfway line, the rest of the boys took up their positions. Kam lifted both his arms indicating exactly where he intended to send the ball. He took two steps forward, swung his left foot and caught the ball perfectly. Barry Payne ran in from the edge of the box and caught the ball beautifully with his left foot, blasting it straight into the bottom right-hand corner of the net. The boys were ecstatic, hugging, and high fiving each other. The All-Star fans went crazy, jumping up and down, Dave and Ade punched the air, "GET IN!!"

The referee blew his whistle and the teams returned to the centre circle once more.

The Dynamos kicked the game off again but immediately the All Stars closed them down and Marc-Bashford, with a sliding tackle, took the ball from their number 10.

Marc-Bashford passed the ball to Raheem Mervyn and the pressure started to build once more. Raheem Mervyn passed the ball to Kam on the left-wing, he dribbled past one player, then another, MEGS! he shouted as he knocked the ball through the defenders legs, he looked up, saw Darnell-Lessi on the edge of the box and struck the ball cleanly, the pass was perfect,

Darnell-Lessi struck it on the volley, the goalkeeper dived but had no chance, the ball flew into the top left hand corner, hitting the back of the net with some force. The Allstars chased Lessi towards the corner flag, Darnell-Lessi turned to Kam and raised both hands,

"Thanks Kam! perfect cross!"

"Thanks, Lessi! perfect finish!" grinned Kam.

After the group celebration, the boys returned to the centre circle and the match continued. The Dynamos pushed and pushed but could not break down the All-Stars defence, after 30 minutes the referee blew his whistle for half time.

The All-Stars entered the dressing room grinning from ear to ear, Dave and Ade couldn't be prouder.

"You were awesome out there! We need more of the same for the second half, they'll have to come to us now so be prepared, concentrate, keep focused and we'll be through to the semi-final, remember, "One team, One dream!"

The All-stars made their way back onto the pitch for the second half, much to the excitement of their fans and the commentators in the television studio.

Ian grinned, "So, Gary how confident are you now? These kids are amazing, I've never seen anything like it in my life, they've only been playing together for such a short time but you'd think they'd grown up together, I can't wait to see what they bring to the second half."

"Well, don't underestimate the Dynamos," replied

Linekar, "I'm sure they'll give these kids a proper game second half, I'm looking forward to this."

The match kicked off again and Dave was right, the Dynamos were more aggressive, pressing the All-Stars every chance they got, nudges off the ball, pulling shirts, attempting to intimidate the confident opposition, but the All-Stars rose to the challenge, they began passing the ball from one player to the next frustrating the Dynamos, Pele-Ali to Payne, Payne to Donaldo, Donaldo made a run down the right-wing when a sliding tackle came in, Arrrgh!! Donaldo fell to the floor clutching his left ankle, the referee blew for a foul and called on the medic. After a couple of minutes, it was obvious Donaldo couldn't continue, and he limped off. Dave waved for Edgar Dravid to come on and take his place, while Kam prepared to take the free kick. He waited for Edgar Dravid to take up his position on the edge of the 18-yard box then took two steps back before whipping the ball into the penalty box. Arnold-Alexander headed it back across the area towards Edgar Dravid, Dravid stepped forward and volleyed the ball past the motionless goalkeeper into the back of the net. The whole stadium erupted, the noise was deafening, the All-Stars ran to their coaches who were jumping for joy on the touchline.

"Big Dave, there's only one Big Dave!" they chanted.

The referee blew again to restart the match and the All-Stars were ready to go again. As soon as the match restarted the ref blew the final whistle and the stadium erupted once again.

Exhausted the All-Stars shook hands with the Dynamos then walked towards their family and friends and more fans than they could ever have hoped for, clapping, thanking them for their support, as they left the pitch they realised it wasn't just their fans that were clapping, above the tunnel they could see the commentators standing at the window of the television studio, clapping, all except Ian Wright, he was jumping up and down, punching the air, shaking his fists with excitement. The All-Stars continued down the tunnel, exhausted but absolutely buzzing with excitement, the dressing room imploded when Dave and Ade entered,

"Big Dave, there's only one Big Dave!"

Ade joined in, "One team, One dream!" Dave stood still, "Just brilliant guys, just brilliant! We're playing Barca Demons in the semi-final guys; they've beaten Paris Youth FC 2 -1.

"Bring it on!" laughed Darnell-Lessi, "We're ready!"

It was going to take a while for the All-Stars to calm down after that performance, but Dave and Ade would see they were fully prepared for their next challenge, the Semi-Final at the Etihad Stadium.

CHAPTER 17

THE SEMI-FINAL

The team coach arrived at the Etihad Stadium to a sea of friends, family and even more fans waving flags and banners, the team looked like professionals in their team tracksuits and fresh haircuts, Brogan had even had the team colours braided into her hair and her blades had had the same treatment, as they left the coach they waved to the excited crowd and Kam blew a kiss to mum,

"That's my boy!" she gushed.

The team made themselves comfortable in the dressing room and changed into their training kits before going on to the pitch for a warmup session. The stadium was filling up quickly and before they knew it, it was time for the big event.

Ade called out, "Right All Stars, back to the dressing room and get changed, I'll announce the team."

The team sat on the benches eager for the team sheet. "OK, I've made a few changes, Barca Demons are a more physical side than Manchester Dynamos so I'm putting some of the bigger lads on, we don't want to get bullied off the ball."

1. Brogan Pitford (goalkeeper)

2. Samuel-Bronson (left-back)

3. Arnold-Alexander (centre-back)

4. Barry Payne (right-back)

5. Pele-Ali (centre-mid)

6. Marc-Bashford (right mid)

7. Kam St. Clair (left-wing)

15. Lemar Jnr (centre-mid).

12. Joe Salah (Striker)

10. Darnell-Lessi (striker)

17. Ethan St. Clair (right-wing)

Subs: 9. Raheem Mervyn, 14. Edgar Dravid, 8. Jacob-Rivermore, 16. Aiden Bayor, 11. Caetano-Donaldo

"Now Barca Demons are a very good side, don't let the last result go to your heads, don't underestimate the opposition, stay strong, keep your shape and talk to each other, sometimes a simple ball is all that's needed so no showing off with the fancy footwork unless it's necessary but above all concentrate, concentrate, concentrate." "COME ON ALL STARS!"

The team stood up and linked their hands above their heads "ALL STARS BY NAME, ALL STARS BY NATURE,

ONE TEAM, ONE DREAM!" then bowed towards Dave and Ade.

They left the dressing room and lined up in the tunnel alongside the Barca Demons. Kam looked up at them, mm! "They are a big team," he thought to himself, "We'll just have to out skill them, there'll be no pushing past these lot. Concentrate, concentrate, concentrate."

As they entered the pitch the noise from the crowd chanting and singing was deafening, flags and banners were waving in every corner of the stadium, the All-Stars fans were the most colourful with their rainbow coloured flags and the loudest, the sound of the African drums were deafening and echoed around the stadium, Dave had called them 'their twelfth man', they really did know how to support their team.

The ref summoned the teams and Kam stood in the centre circle ready for kick off......the ref put the whistle to his mouth and blew.

Kam passed the ball to Pele-Ali who ran to the edge of the centre circle with the ball, Lemar Jr had made a run down the middle but this was just to confuse the Demons, two of their defenders swooped on him leaving a clear pass open to Ethan St. Clair who had sprinted down the right-wing, he took one touch and crossed the ball high into the penalty area, the goalkeeper came out but was too slow, Joe Salah leaped high into the air to meet the pass and headed it back across goal to Darnell-Lessi, the goalkeeper was struggling to get back and Lessi headed the ball toward the bottom right corner, the goalkeeper scrambling to reach it but he had no chance "GOAL! YESSSSS!" jumping, punching the air, the All-Stars ran to congratulate him, Brogan was doing her usual little shimmy on the penalty spot as she did for all the All-Stars goals, Dave, and Ade high fived each other, and the ref blew to call the teams back to restart the game.

The pundits in the TV studio were in total shock, Ian was his usual excitable self "I love this team, superb team goal, and only 2 minutes on the clock, it's better than watching Champions League!"

"I wouldn't go that far," laughed Rio.

"Why not, these kids are playing for the love of the game and each other, not millions of pounds. It's how it should be!" smiled Ian.

Kam stood on the edge of the centre circle, "Concentrate now guys! Come on, we can do this!" The ref blew his whistle and the game started once more.

The Demons kicking off this time spent the next fifteen minutes pushing and pushing the All-Stars to the limit but each time getting blocked by the All-Stars midfield players, eventually passing the ball back through the midfield and back to their goalkeeper, with Joe Salah sprinting towards him the goalkeeper quickly ran on to the ball and kicked it high up the pitch.

Brogan, backing into her goal shouted, "Samuel, pick up the winger!" but it was too late, the winger ran on to the goal keepers ball, the Demons had flooded the box already, just in time for him to put the cross in, Arnold-Alexander ran towards the edge of the box to cut out the cross but missed the ball and caught the heel of their number 9's boot, number 9 fell to the floor. "Penalty!"

Arnold-Alexander held his head in his hands and the referee pointed to the spot. The Demons supporters rose to their feet, jumping up and down, cheering and shouting, their no.9 picked up the ball and placed it on the penalty spot. Brogan spat on her gloves, rubbing her hands together, whilst giving the penalty taker the meanest look she could. Constantly moving from side to side, waving her arms around, the no.9 turned and walked away from the ball before turning for his run-up, he moved towards the ball slowly before swinging his right foot forcing the ball towards the top left corner, Brogan, sprang into action, she flew as if she had wings, like a bird, stretching, clipping the ball with her fingertips pushing it over the bar, she landed in a heap at the bottom of the post. The All-Stars ran to her, hardly believing what she had just done, picking her up, Kam looked a little concerned.

"You ok Brogan, didn't get hurt, did you?"

Brogan winking "Who me? Told you I'm tougher than I look, didn't I?"

"That's my girl" Kam blushed.

"Got that right Kam," she replied, Kam blushed some more. 'Pull yourself together, she's just a girl,' he smiled to himself.

"Mark up, Mark up!" Dave was bellowing from the touchline; the Demons were about to take the corner.

Brogan ready on the goal line once again, Arnold-Alexander on the far post, everyone man making their opposing player, the ball swooped in, Bashford headed out as far as the edge of the area, it dropped nicely for their no.10. He looked up and struck the ball towards goal, Brogan diving to her right felt a tug on her jersey, she was being held back by the demons' center-forward, the ball flew past her and into the bottom right-hand corner, the Demons had scored, the referee ignored the protests from the All-Stars and allowed the goal. Boos echoed around the stadium from the All-Stars fans and the All-Stars players' heads dropped. The referee blew for half time and the players made their way down the tunnel. The Demons were smirking and winking at them as they walked back to the dressing rooms, Brogan almost in tears was furious, "Come on All-Stars! We're not going to let a team like this one wind us up, are we?"

The boys looked at each other and began to smile, Ethan kissed the badge on his chest, and shouted at the top of his voice, "One team, one dream!" and no-one but no-one is going to stop us lifting that trophy!"

The boys entered the dressing room, grabbed a drink each, and sat down for the half time pep talk.

"Well boys, I have to say you were robbed of the lead, they cheated I know but for the next half an hour keep playing as you have been, and you've got nothing to worry about." "And as for you Brogan, well what can I say A-M-A-Z-I-N-G!" "I'm so proud of you, that save was world class!"

"Yeah, I know it was," she grinned, everyone laughed, "Brogan! Brogan!" they chanted. Dave waved his arms, "Ok, Ok, now that you've all calmed down, I want you to go back out onto that pitch, heads held high and show them how to really play this beautiful game, with grace and honesty, with pride and determination."

"YES BOSS!"

The second half both teams had chances to go ahead but it seemed both goalkeepers were in top form, each denying the opposing team from going ahead, the All-Stars won a throw-in just past the halfway line and with five minutes to go Dave decided to make a substitution, bringing Aiden Bayor on for Barry Payne. It was a risk taking off a defender for an attacking player but only scoring was going to see them through to the final. Payne got a standing ovation as he came off and the crowd cheered on Aiden Bayor. He took up his position just behind Darnell-Lessi and Joe Salah.

Marc-Bashford threw the ball to Pele-Ali, Pele-Ali turned and nutmegged one player, took it around a second, chipped it over another and ran straight towards goal, with two players running towards him he passed the ball to Kam on his left-hand side, Kam flew down the wing, knocked it past the last defender and ran to the edge of the area, Darnell-Lessi, Jo Salah and Aiden Bayor were all racing into the area, Kam looked up and hit it first time across goal, too quick for Lessi, not far enough for Jo Salah, but right on cue for Aiden Bayor, a left-foot volley the ball screamed past the stunned goalkeeper into the roof of the net. The stadium erupted, the fans screaming with delight, the All-Stars boys ran to Brogan and began to shimmy, much to her delight,

"You guys, you're crazy!"

"Yeah, crazy for this team!" laughed Darnell-Lessi. The referee blew his whistle, the Demons were eager to kick off again.

A minute to go. The All-Stars needed to keep their nerve for 60 more seconds, Kam intercepted a pass and ran with the ball to the corner flag, two players on his back trying to take the ball from him, he needed all his strength to hold them back, he backheeled the ball and it took a deflection, he'd won a corner.

Ethan ran over, "Kam! Kam! take a short one,"

Kam tapped the ball to Ethan, now it was his turn to take the ball back to the corner flag, putting his foot on top of the ball, rolling it back and forth........and the final whistle blew. "We did it bro!" laughed Kam hugging his brother, "And to think it used to be so annoying having a little brother following me around everywhere now look at us, we're on our way to the world cup final!"

They walked towards the rest of team arms around each other shoulders, grinning from ear to ear, Dave and Ade ran onto the pitch, fist-pumping each player in turn, they lifted Brogan onto their shoulders and walked with the boys over to their fans behind the goal.

"ALL-STAR! ALL-STARS!" The fans chanted,

"Big Dave! There's only one Big Dave!" Dave turned to see the All-Stars had lined up, arms around each other's shoulders singing at the top of their voices, the fans joined in,

"Big Dave! There's only one Big Dave!" and those happy tears were flowing once again. Kam wrapped his arms around Dave's waist and squeezed,

"Thanks boss, for everything, for believing in us, we did it, we actually did it!"

Dave looked down, "Well done son! you did it, you all did it, you believed in yourselves, that's why we're in the World Cup Final next week, the hard work paid off." Kam's eyes filled up but didn't quite overflow, he'd noticed Brogan watching him.

"You ok, Brogan? You've not picked up any injuries I hope? We've got another big match coming up in case you hadn't heard," he grinned.

"I'm fine Kam, thanks to you lot I didn't have a lot to do, did I? Well apart from those amazing saves I made, told you I was good, didn't I?" she chuckled.

"Good? Good? You were AMAZING!", he winked.

The All-Stars waved to their fans as they left the pitch, "See you at Wembley!" they shouted as they headed towards the tunnel, and the chants continued........

   "All-STARS!   ALL-STARS!"

Mum, Diego and Ano, Esme, Evan-Havard, Bako, and Nala, were all waiting in the dressing room,

"Yay! here they are, our young superstars!" shouted Bako as they arrived, after lots of hugging and embarrassing kisses from Mum, Kam and the team showered and changed back into their tracksuits and climbed back onto the coach. "Who've we got in the final boss?" shouted Ethan"

You ready boys? Drum roll please," laughed Ade, "the result of the other semi-final was, after a long pause, Ade took a deep breath and shouted:

"CHELSKI UTD 2.........LIVERPOOL AVENGERS.........1!"

The response was deafening ...."YESSSSSS!" BRING IT ON JOSEPH ROMENIO, BRING IT ON!"

"WEMBLY HERE WE COME!!!!"

CHAPTER 18

THE FINAL

The day had finally arrived, Cup Final day, the coach arrived on time at the Community Centre and the boys arrived one by one excited but looking a little nervous about the big game ahead. It was quieter than usual on the road to Wembley, looking round Dave hoped the occasion wasn't going to be too much for them especially as they were playing last years' winners, Chelski Utd. They were the current world champions.

Their fans didn't disappoint though, the All Stars arrived at Wembley Stadium to an amazing scene of flags, banners and scarves waving around above what seemed like a crowd of a million people shouting, calling their name, it was the lift the team needed, their eyes lit up.

Brogan stood up first "Right you guys, you see all those people out there, they believe in us, Dave and Ade believe in us, and I believe in us! So, come on let's get this show on the road and show Chelski Utd exactly what we're made of and bring that cup home where it belongs, in Well Borne!"

The boys stood up clapping and cheering.

Kam patted Brogan on her back, "Thanks Brogan I think we all needed that."

He turned to the boys and shouted, "The only reason Chelski Utd are champions is because our team didn't exist last year. BUT WE'RE HERE NOW!" The coach erupted with cheers and high fiving, "COME ON ALL-STARS!"

As they entered the changing room the All Stars were buzzing with excitement, Dave pinned the team sheet to the notice board:

1. Brogan Pitford (goalkeeper)

2. Samuel-Bronson (left-back)

3. Arnold-Alexander (centre-back)

4. Barry Payne (right-back)

5. Pele-Ali (centre-mid)

6. Tevin Dejoyner (right mid)

7. Kam St. Clair (left-wing)

16. Aiden Bayor (right mid)

12. Joe Salah (Striker)

10. Darnell-Lessi (striker)

17. Ethan St. Clair (right-wing)

Subs: 6. Marc-Bashford 9. Raheem Mervyn, 14. Edgar Dravid, 8. Jacob-Rivermore, 15. Lemar Jnr. 11. Caetano-Donaldo

There was no disappointment. Everyone including the substitutes knew they had a part to play on this momentous occasion. Everyone quickly changed into their kit, boots were laced up, shin pads in place, and they were raring to go. Dave called the team together and put his hands together as if he were about to pray.

"Right All Stars, listen up! All I'm going to say is, we've trained hard for this day, you've got the knowledge, the confidence, the skills and determination to succeed today, but more importantly you've got the belief, the friendship, the love and respect for each other and that's the reason you're on the verge of winning The World Cup, you've got it all because you've got each other!, now go out there and bring that cup home!"

The room was silent for all of two seconds ....

"YES BOSS", "YES GAFFA", "C'MON ALL-STARS, WE'VE GOT THIS" "ALL-STARS BY NAME, ALL-STARS BY NATURE!"

Dave grinned "Love you guys!"

Ade put his arm around Dave's shoulder, "You ok brother?"

Dave smiled, "I'm good, you know, no matter what happens now, win or lose I couldn't be any prouder than I am right now."

The teams lined up in the tunnel, Kam in front alongside the Chelski captain, they shook hands and walked out onto the pitch. The stadium was full and the noise from both sets of fans cheering on their team was deafening, blue and white flags, scarves, and banners for Chelski and rainbow colours for the All-Stars, confetti spilled out from the All-Star fans like a rainbow-coloured rain,

Wembley just looked magical. The referee placed the ball on the podium and the teams lined up, side by side. The teams paraded past each other and shook hands, then ran towards their respective goals for a last-minute practice before the referee blew the whistle for them to take their positions for kick-off, Chelski were first to kick off.

The goalkeepers raised their hands to say they were ready, and the ref blew his whistle.

Chelski hit a long ball over the All-Stars midfield towards the runner on the left but Barry Payne intercepted for the All-Stars, he passed the ball towards Kam on the left-wing, Kam picked up the pass, looked up and attempted to pass the ball to Pele-Ali, but the pass was short, Kam could do nothing but watch the Chelski no.9 pick up the ball on the edge of the 18 yd box and shoot. The ball flew towards goal at superfast speed but Brogan was ready as always, she dived to her left, the ball got closer and closer, but then the worst thing happened, the ball took a deflection off Arnold-Alexander as he'd jumped for the ball, the ball swerved to the right, Brogan tried to get back but the ball hit the back of the net, the Chelski players were jumping all over each other and their fans went crazy......

Chelski 1 - All-Stars 0

After just two minutes this was not the start the All-Stars had hoped for or expected.

137

Brogan sat in the middle of the goal, angry, punching the floor, Arnold-Alexander and Payne helped her up,

"Sorry Brogan, we should have stopped him before he took a shot,"

"Kam ran over to make sure she was ok, "My fault guys, the pass was too short, I should have done better,"

Brogan stood up "Will you guys stop that, blaming yourselves, we're a team, you idiots, it's no-one's fault, now stop wasting time, c'mon, we go again!"

"Wow, thought my mum was bossy," laughed Kam.

"Yes, Kam I am bossy, and you're the captain so go and do what captain's do and lead this team to victory!"

Kam kicked the game off for the second time, and for the next quarter of an hour Chelski were impossible to break down, the Chelski boys were bigger and stronger and were so desperate to hold on to the lead that they hardly attempted to get a second goal, as if they thought they'd won already.

But then things went from bad to worse, Brogan rolled the ball out to Barry Payne, Payne passed it sideways to Arnold-Alexander, but Arnold-Alexander wasn't ready, and the ball went out for a Chelski throw-in level with the 18 yd box. Chelski pushed up, and the All-Stars midfielders and Kam and Ethan came back to defend the throw leaving only Lessi on the halfway line. The Chelski winger picked up the ball and took a few steps back and lifted the ball over his head. He charged towards the line and thew the ball with all his might, the ball flew into the penalty area, "I've got it!" shouted Payne, but just as he went to jump he felt someone tugging at his shirt and his feet never left the ground, the Chelski centre-forward had run in from the edge of the area and with Payne unable to challenge him he rose into the air and caught the ball perfectly, heading it past Brogan into the bottom left corner. The Chelski team huddled together to congratulate each other, an appeal for a foul on Payne to the referee fell on deaf ears and the goal stood.

Chelski 2 All-Stars 0.

The All-Stars' heads dropped, even Brogan looked ready to burst into tears.

"Heads up guys!" bellowed Dave from the touchline. "It's not over yet, you can do this!"

They walked heads bowed towards the centre circle, the ref blew his whistle and Kam passed the ball to Pele-Ali, but there was no time the ref blew for half time.

Kam walked towards his coach, he saw the pain in Dave's eyes and Kam's eyes began to fill up, partly because they were losing but mostly because he felt he was letting 'Big Dave' down. At that very moment, he realised he'd come to love this giant of a man, this kind, gentle giant who had become like a father to him, he knew how much this rainbow team meant to Dave and all the hard work he'd put in. "Right, that's it!" he thought to himself, "Second half Chelski are going to wonder what's hit them."

Heading back down the tunnel to the dressing room the Chelski players were laughing and poking fun at the All-Stars, "Champions! Champions! Don't bother coming back out for the second half, you'll be wasting your time!" they laughed.

Kam had to hold back Brogan, she looked ready for a fight, "Leave it Brogan, we'll do our fighting on the pitch second half," Brogan gritted her teeth, stomped her feet, and marched angrily into the dressing room.

Dave waited for them to all take a drink and be seated and then began his half-time team talk.

"Right, we're 2-0 down, and look at you all are sitting there feeling sorry for yourselves, you look like you've lost already, but if they can score two goals in half an hour, guess what? we can too, in fact we can score three. Remember when I told you that there's a time and a place for fancy footwork and show-off skills? Well, today's the day. These boys are big and strong, and they're using their strength to their full advantage. Now, you guys are the most talented, the most skillful players I have ever seen, the only way you'll beat this Chelski side is by using your biggest strength to your advantage! They may be bigger, but you're faster and more skillful by far, so pass the ball quicker, just pass it and run, pass it, and run. Don't give them time to knock you off the ball.

Their centre -forward is their best player, he stands out

from the rest, but they rely on him, I'm going to bring Jacob-Rivermore and Edgar Dravid on for Pele-Ali and Dejoyner, your job is to stop their midfield from passing the ball to him and Caetano-Donaldo and Raheem Mervyn are on for Barry Payne and Arnold-Alexander, you need to stick to that player like glue, don't give him an inch. With him out of the picture they'll struggle, and we haven't tested the goalkeeper yet so let's see what he's made of. Stop trying to walk the ball into the net, if you see a gap, shoot! I've seen some superb long-distance goals on the training ground, now let's see some more."

The All-Stars stood up, linked hands, and lifted them above their heads, "All-Stars by name, All-Stars by nature, COME ON ALL-STARS!"

They strutted down the tunnel grinning from ear to ear, much to the surprise of the Chelski players, except for Brogan of course, she growled at any player that looked her way. Kam smiled to himself 'That's my girl!'

The All-Stars kicked off for the second half, Kam tapped the ball sideways to Rivermore, Rivermore passed the ball to Aiden-Bayor on the right of midfield, who took the ball around one player, then another, Ethan had made a run down the right wing and shouted to him to pass him the ball, and that's exactly what he did, Ethan caught the ball cleanly and ran to the by-line, he stopped and looked up and saw Kam racing towards goal, Ethan crossed the ball with his right foot across goal, Kam had timed his run perfectly, he caught the ball on his left foot before it could even touch the ground, it flew straight into the right top corner, the goalkeeper had no chance, his first goal of the tournament and it was superb!"

Chelski 2 - All-Stars 1.

He ran to Ethan who was punching the air, grabbing him, hugged him and planted the biggest, squishiest kiss on his forehead.

"Thanks bro!" laughed Ethan, "I knew you loved me really," the rest of the team caught up, and the hugging continued. Kam turned to look for Brogan, she was jumping up and down, screaming, she gave Kam a thumbs-up with both hands and Kam returned the gesture. The stadium had erupted, the All -Stars fans were hysterical, flags swaying from side to side, children screaming, the villagers who were right at the front, were singing and dancing and jumping up and down, Wembley was just a wall of noise. Kam looked over at Dave running up and down the touchline, punching the air and high fiving Ade, Kam's stomach flipped over with pride, he looked around the stadium, he couldn't help thinking, 'I've got a good feeling about this, I think today is going to be a good day.' He picked up the ball and ran back to the centre- circle, no time to lose.

The teams returned to the centre-circle and Chelski kicked the game off again.

Chelski Utd. were looking worried, and they had every

need to be, the All-Stars were rampaging, chasing every ball, blocking every pass, keeping Chelski well and truly trapped in their own half, then the magic began to happen......

Kam picked up the ball on the halfway line, with a player running towards him he flicked the ball up, turned his back and chipped it over the on-coming player, a quick turn, he gave the defender the slip, ran onto the ball and headed for goal, the next defender stood his ground..."MEGS!" he shouted as he put the ball through his legs, only the goalkeeper to beat now, he slowed down, picked his spot, waited for the goalkeeper to make his move and BANG! bottom left corner, GOALLLL!!!!!

Chelski 2 All-Stars 2.

Kam stood still and took a bow before he was almost flattened by the rest of his team jumping on his back. Once again, the crowd erupted, "This kid' is unbelievable!" He overheard one of the Chelski players say, but Kam kept his cool, kept focused, picked up the ball and ran back to the centre circle, with five minutes to go the pressure was on.

After they had kicked off again Chelski knew they needed to push forward and try and stop the awesome All-Stars getting the winner. Chelski won a free kick halfway into the All-Stars half after a clumsy challenge from Caetano. Ten yards in front of the ball, the All-

Stars created a wall of four with Caetano, Mervyn, Livermore, and Dravid.

Brogan was shouting to them to make sure she could see the ball, everyone took up their defensive positions and the ref blew his whistle, the ball came in high over the wall, right on to the penalty spot Samuel-Bronson got there first, as his foot reached the ball the unthinkable happened.....he slipped and the ball swerved in the opposite direction to where Brogan had been guarding her goal, the ball trickled over the line much to the delight of Chelski and their fans.

Chelski 3 - All-Stars 2.

But the All-Stars weren't beaten yet, Ethan ran back to the centre circle with the ball, and they were ready to go again. Chelski took their time, trying to waste precious time before the referee blew his whistle and shouted for them to hurry up, stopping his watch until they were ready.

Right from the off, Lessi sent a long ball down the left wing for Kam to chase but the Chelski defender kicked it out for a throw-in. Jo Salah picked up the ball and took a long throw into the penalty area, Lessi was on the end of it, he took the ball around one player with ease and hit it hard towards goal, but the goalkeeper did well and managed to scramble across and push it around the post for an All-Star corner. The crowd roared, "COME ON ALL-STARS! COME ON ALL-STARS!"

Caetano stepped up to take the corner and lifted his right hand to signify where he was going to put the ball. The All-Stars found themselves looking up at the Chelski defenders, it was going to be almost impossible to jump higher than this lot. Then Kam had an idea,

"Hey Ethan, remember when we were watching rugby the other day and we talked about that thing?"

Ethan looked around and winked "Yeah, I remember." Kam called over Aiden Bayor and whispered something in his ear, they were ready, Kam and Aiden Bayor stood either side of Ethan (the smallest player on the pitch), Caetano took a few steps back then stepped forward and hooked the ball past the first defender, Kam shouted to Aiden Bayor "Ok, go!" As the ball came over it seemed as if Caetano had hit it too high, but this was deliberate, Kam and Aiden Bayor grabbed a leg each and lifted Ethan head and shoulders above the rest just as they do in rugby, the ball was perfect for Ethan, he headed it downwards, it bounced in front of the goalkeeper, under his legs and straight down the middle of the goal!! "GET IN!" Ethan was beside himself; he was being pulled in every direction by his teammates, laughing hysterically, he hugged his big brother.

"You're the best Kam!"

"No, you're the best Ethan!"

"No, you're the best Kam"!

"Ok, ok you two," laughed Lessi, to save the argument I'll be the best!"

Chelski 3 - All-Stars 3.

With only two minutes of extra time to go it was now or never, Chelski kicked off and sent a long ball towards the All-Stars 18 yd box, Brogan was ready though, she ran out and kicked the ball as hard as she could, it reached Raheem Mervyn, he headed the ball back over his head, onto Caetano who had his back to goal, he held up the Chelski defender until Kam flew past him, Caetano back-heeled the ball to Kam and he was racing toward goal, nearer and nearer he went and then..........a defender stuck out his foot and Kam came crashing down, "Arrgh my leg" the referee blew his whistle and Kam heard "PENALTY!" The adrenalin kicked in and suddenly the leg pain disappeared. Try as they might the Chelski players complained to the referee that it was accidental, but the referee pointed to the spot again.

Darnell-Lessi picked up the ball and placed it on the penalty spot. The Chelski goalkeeper took his place and began to move side to side trying to put Lessi off. But Lessi kept his concentration, turned his back to goal and took a few steps back then turned to face the goal.   A short run and he hit the ball full force towards goal.....but the goalkeeper guessed right and got his fingertips to the ball, pushing the ball up, it hit the bar, Kam turned away putting his head in his hands, not believing he'd saved it, he looked up and saw Brogan pointing, shouting, he looked up and saw the ball coming over the top of him, he leaned back just in time, swiveled slightly to his left and caught the ball perfectly with his right foot, he smashed it over his head towards goal, through one player, then another, the goalkeeper wasn't expecting it.... didn't see it......it flew straight down the centre of the goals hitting the back of the net, Kam dropped to his knees, hardly believing what he'd just done, Ethan and Lessi dragged him to his feet and the rest of the team ran and lifted him onto their shoulders, "KING KAM! KING KAM! WOW! WOW! WOW!"

Chelski 3 - All Stars 4!!

The ref blew to restart the game, but Dave made a tactical decision, he called to the ref he wanted to make a substitution. On came Marc-Bashford and Lemar Jr. and off went Aiden Bayor and Joe Salah. The match restarted, Chelski kicked a long ball, and the referee blew his whistle for the final time, they had done it, they had actually done it, they had won the World Cup! Kam ran and picked up the match ball, "I think this belongs to me!" he shouted.

Dave and Ade ran onto the pitch, followed closely by Mum and Esme, as Dave reached Kam he lifted him, throwing him high into the air, "Told you Kam, told you we'd score three, but you had to go one better didn't you and score four!", he laughed, by now the tears were rolling down Dave's cheek, "Those happy tears back are they Dave" cried Kam

"Looks like it,"

Dave laughed wiping the tears from his face.

"Hey Mum, told you I'd be King of the World one day, didn't I? Mum smothered him in kisses before turning to Ethan to dish out some more. By now the All-Stars family and friends were on the pitch, Wembley felt like the happiest place in the world right now. Kam looked round for Brogan, he spotted her, celebrating with her family, he ran over and gave her a hug.

"You were awesome today, Kam!", Kam puffed out his chest and laughed

 "I know I was," he laughed, Brogan punched his arm playfully.

"Ouch!" Kam laughed, "what was that for?"

"You're so funny, Kam,"

"You were great today too Brogan, who needs feet when you have wings to fly! I think you're amazing," Kam began to blush when he realised what he'd said.

"I think I'm amazing too!" laughed Brogan, "And you're pretty cool too," now they were both blushing.

"Where's Diego and Ano mum? asked Ethan,

"Don't worry about that, they have a surprise for you, just wait, and see.

Joseph Romenio walked over to Dave and Ade and

shook their hands. "You know what guys, I always believed I was the best football manager in the world, you know 'special' and that I'd got the best team in the world, but you guys you are the special ones, really, really special, well done, you were amazing out there." With a tear in his eye, he joined the Chelski players, who were looking tired and a little glum at losing, they shook hands and congratulated the All-Stars before climbing the steps to receive their runners up medals.

Then it was time for Dave, Ade and Evan-Havard and the All-Stars to climb the steps, one by one they climbed, higher and higher, hugging, and high five-Ing the crowd as they passed, some giving them their caps and scarves, by the time they reached the top the All-Stars were wrapped in the scarves and banners of their adoring, amazing, happy fans.

They walked along the gantry where they were greeted by The President of the Football Association, Princess Charlotte, she shook hands and placed a winner's medals around each player, all except Kam, the last to receive his medal, he got a peck on the cheek too, much to Brogans annoyance, and then the moment he'd only dreamed of, Princess Charlotte winked at him, "You ready Kam?"

"You bet I am!" shouted Kam.

Princess Charlotte gently placed the Youth World Cup in Kam's hands, Kam turned to face the crowd........"YAAAAAY!" he lifted the cup high above his head, the crowd roared and cheered, banners waving, drums banging, trumpets playing, the sight in front of him was overwhelming, Kam's tears streaming down his face, but he didn't care, he was so, so, happy, he passed the cup to Brogan, she lifted it to more cheers, she passed it to Pele-Ali who passed it along the line until each and every player had lifted the cup, and then they made their way back down to the pitch where they were greeted by a sea of reporters and camera flashes.

As they stood for a team photograph, music began blaring throughout the stadium.

Kam looked at Ethan "I recognise that tune, that's one of Diego and Ano creations." They looked over towards the dugout and there, much to their surprise, was Diego and Ano.

"Whoa! What is going on? and .... is that who I think it is or am I dreaming"? beamed Ethan. "It's Will, It's Will, Will-I-Am is there, over there with my brother!"

Grinning from ear to ear, Diego waved to his brothers, picked up the microphone and handed it to Will. Diego, Ano, and Will stepped forward onto the pitch and into the centre circle, and the stadium fell silent.

"Good evening, everyone!" shouted Will, "Let me introduce you to my new friends Diego and Ano, I've been working with these two talented guys for a while now, ever since they started posting their music on YouTube. We've created a few tracks together and I'm super impressed with the way they've turned out. One day we were chatting online when they told me about this 'football ' team that Diego's brothers play for, how they've come together from different parts of the world to pursue their dream of playing at the World Cup finals. Now I don't understand this game we call soccer in the USA, but I do understand that it takes a lot of hard work and commitment to fulfill your dreams in whatever you choose to do. So, we've created this piece of music to say well done to you, your coaches and to everyone who helped to make these amazing kids' dream come true. And to you, 'All-Stars' we never doubted for one minute that you wouldn't lift that cup, you guys are DOPE!!"

The All-Stars stood side by side, arms around each other's shoulders, Brogan in the centre between Kam and Ethan, Mum linked arms with Dave, Evan-Havard sitting on Dave's shoulders, alongside Ade and Esme. Diego and Ano signaled to each other, and the music started up again and Will-I-Am, Diego and Ano began:

"No matter who you are or where you come from,

If we only have one thing in common, we can become one.

Start a conversation, create a foundation, make friends,

talk, walk, dance, sing, play sport, together, start new trends,

Like each other, love each other, show respect,

Help each other, learn from each other to be the best.

There's only one world, embrace it, cherish it and everyone on it,

You can do it, we can do it, together we are better, this place is 'LIT!"

The stadium began to sway to the music, from the reporters, the cameramen, the ball boys, Joseph Romenio, the Chelski team, everyone joined in, the TV pundits had come down onto the pitch to join in the fun, "Look at Ian," laughed Kam, "He's really getting his groove on!"

"No matter who you are or where you come from,

If we only have one thing in common, we can become one.

Start a conversation, create a foundation, make friends,

talk, walk, dance, sing, play sport, together, start new trends,

Like each other, love each other, show respect,

Help each other, learn from each other, be the best.

There's only one world, embrace it, cherish it and everyone on it,

You can do it, we can do it, together we are better, this place is 'LIT!"

The stadium erupted in celebration, supporters from both teams embraced each other, the competition was over, new friendships had begun and would continue long after this day to remember had ended. It was clear to see why this game, this beautiful game is a global phenomenon, it has far-reaching effects beyond sport, the possibilities to change the world are endless when everyone comes together for each other........

The boys went to the World Cup Final at Wembley Stadium that summer as guests of honour, they got to meet their heroes, the best players in the world, they had the best time, but it never could compare to the day they won their own World Cup, the Real World Cup where the world actually came together to create the best youth team ever and as for Kam, well, King Kam as he was known from that day on, he really was living his best life!

THE END

Kam, Ethan, Diego, Ano, Jacob, Aiden, Rio, Zach, Samuel, Dravid and the amazing Evan and Brogan are all real children (these are their real first names) and are known to me.

Brogan really does wear prosthetics and continues to play football, recently scoring four goals in one match.......

These truly amazing children inspired me to write this book and my dream is for you to be equally inspired to follow your dreams because they really can come true.